PINK MOON RISING

PINK MOON RISING

Pieces of Jane

HALSTEN SKÖLD HUTCHINGS

Halsten Sköld Hutchings

Author's Note

When I learned that Indigenous women and girls go missing at alarming rates, I was shocked and heartbroken. *Pink Moon Rising; Pieces of Jane* is my way of dealing with this and doing something about it. My goal is to present Jane's story in a respectful way and to show women and girls who have been trafficked that they are seen. The poems and free verse segments in *Pink Moon Rising* are pieces of Jane's life. There is much more to her story; her heritage and Indigenous family are subjects for another book. While Jane and I are different in many ways, we have the same desire to belong and to be seen.

Dedication
To the invisible.

I

PROLOGUE
STORY OF THE COYOTE AND THE MOON

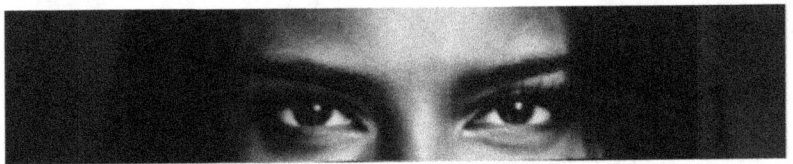

The Coyote and The Moon

(Based on a Native American story.)

I haven't seen my mother for many
years.
But the stories she told me are vivid.
Especially
The Coyote *and The Moon.*

Once upon a time,
there was the Moon.

Moon was always very beautiful.
Sometimes,
she was gold like a sunflower or metallic silver
or blue.
Other times she was a shade of pink or red
like blood.
There was also Coyote.
He was as swift as the leaves blowing in the
cold autumn wind.
Coyote lived in Spirit World.
Lastly,
there was the sun,
a fireball in the sky...
orange and in some places,
a vibrant rosy red in others.
They all lived in harmony,

except,
Sun was in love with Moon.
So was Coyote.
Sun was furious with this because
Moon was stunning.
During a warm summer's day in late June,
Sun came up with a plan to make Moon
fall in love and forget about Coyote.
The next day,
as Coyote was gathering goods for Moon in
Spirit World,
Sun said,

"Hey there,

Coyote,
you know that Moon prefers goods from Earth,
why don't you give her some goods from Earth?"
He tried to get out of Spirit World.
He did.
There was a problem;
once you leave Spirit World you cannot return
to your place of rest,
you become a ghost.
However,
Coyote didn't know about that.
When Coyote tried to return,
he was locked out.
From that day on,
Coyote can be seen wandering
Earth and every night he howls up at Moon telling

her he loves her and
will
return

       to

            her

                one

                    day.

              The End.

The

moon

sees

you.

The moon sees me.

PART ONE

PINK MOON FALLING

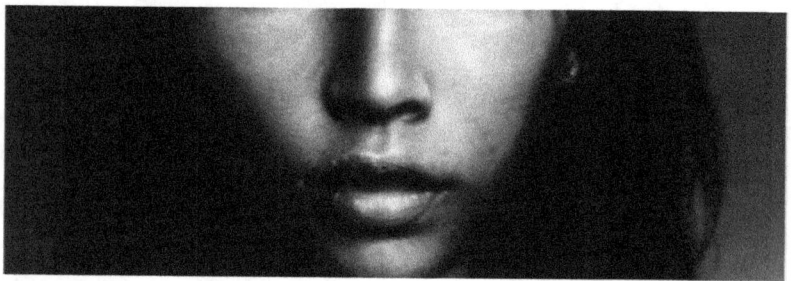

I am Jane.
I am a daughter.
I am a friend.
I am a loved one.
I am somebody.
I am not seen.

Invisible as Air ☾ Jane Nocona

is how I feel.
Sure,
people do look at me.
Some even *stare*.
I don't care.
To me,
it's better to be stared at than not to be seen
at all.
I just want to be seen.
Is this too much to ask?

Wind in My Hair ☾ *Jane Nocona*
July 27, 2021
Omaha, NE
6 am

When I get up in the morning,
it feels like I am the only one in the world,
except for the sun,
just the sun and me.
Before anyone else is up, I go out for a run.
I love the feeling of the cold morning
breeze on my face and the rush of
adrenaline through my veins.
I love the feeling of wind in my hair.
Whenever I run I feel like
me.

A MEMORY

JULY 6TH, 2010

OMAHA, NEBRASKA

☾

The Writing on the Wall ☾ Jane Nocona

I've heard *countless* stories of Indigenous
women and girls going missing and being
murdered.
They are true and tragic stories.
I was young when I first heard these stories.
I probably thought–
I don't know what I thought.
Maybe I thought it was from a plot line in
American Horror Story.
I was much too young to understand.
I didn't fully grasp it until I was fourteen
or maybe fifteen.
The scariest thing about them is that every
last one reminds me of my friend,
Clara....
and me.

It was in June,
midsummer.
I was going on an evening walk.
I usually went alone,
but this time I had a friend.
Clara was eighteen.
I was twelve at the time.

I never saw or heard from her again after
that night.

She's probably dead...
somewhere,
just lying there.
I miss Clara immensely.

We were walking around Omaha.
All of the sudden,
something red caught my eye.
I showed it to Clara.
She looked up.
It read...

MMIWG.

2

She fell silent.
She was much older and more mature than I
was.

"What does MMIWG mean?"
I asked.
She abruptly became very sad.
She took a deep breath.
I didn't mean to make her sad.

"You'll learn when you are older."
We both continued to stare at the red graffiti.
M.
M.
I.
W.
G.
Clara took a deep breath.
She sniffled,
and I looked over at her.
She looked at me.

She sighed.

A sad sigh.

"I guess
I can tell you a little about it,
Jane.
You remember Lucile,
don't you?"
I nodded.

"Of course I do."

"Well,
remember when she left that one day?"
I nodded.

"She never came back.
No one noticed and no one cared that she
was gone.
I make it a point to remember her...
Jane,
When I leave tomorrow,
I want you to remember me because if you
don't,
no one will.
Not even Lydia."

"I won't ever forget you,
Clara."
A sad smile spread across her face.
She sighed.
She hugged me.
I hugged her back.

"I know you won't, Jane.

You are impossible to forget,
and it's a tragedy that you feel 'invisible'.
Trust me,
you aren't invisible,"
she said,
smiling slightly.
    "If you won't forget about me,
I won't forget about you."

JULY 6, 2010

IN THE LIVING ROOM AT THE SHELTER

OMAHA, NEBRASKA

☾

I am a curious person,
of course.
Being curious is both a blessing and curse.
I remember spending hours searching on the
computer in the kitchen.
I was staying with the family that took care
of Clara and me for a few months.
I distinctly remember that it was pitch black
that night.
The brightness of the screen was glaring in my
eyes.
I typed
    "what does MMIWG mean?"
What I saw sent shivers down my spine.
For as long as I live,
until my dying day,
I'll never forget what I saw.
    "MMIWG stands for Missing and Murdered
Indigenous Women and Girls.
Indigenous Women and Girls face violence at rates
that are much higher than the national average."
I stared and rubbed my eyes.
I looked back.
I blinked.
Twice.
One.
Two.
I did not believe what I read.
I could not believe what I read.

I felt as if I had opened a Pandora's Box.
I did.
I did.

I read on.

3

The more I read,
the more I understood...
It all made sense-
why Clara always insisted on going with me
on my early morning and early evening walks
around the Old Market and why she was so
scared.
I knew I should have stopped reading,
but I couldn't.
Footsteps soon interrupted my search.
Somehow,
I knew it was Clara.
    "Clara?"
    "Jane,
where are you?"
    "In the kitchen,"
I said.
She walked in.
I tipped my head up to look at her.

"Why didn't you tell me sooner about all the
women and girls missing and murdered who are
just.
Like.
Us?"
Clara sighed.
"Look,
Jane,
I didn't want to tell you because I didn't want to
scare you.
But,
I am going to tell you because I don't want you to
learn
the hard way like I did."
I stared.
I knew there was more...
I just knew.
"I've experienced violence,
and I feel responsible for protecting you from the
violence that girls like you and I face."
"I-
I'm sorry, Clara."
Clara looked at me as if she were a million miles
away.
"W-
will it happen to me?"
She didn't respond to my question.
But she continued to look directly at me.
"Please,

just promise me one thing,
Jane."
   "Okay,"
I said,
looking worried.
   "Just be careful out there,
Jane.
Take care of yourself,
please.
Men can be very dangerous,
so can women.
Choose your friends carefully.
They can lead you to a crazy train that will
destroy you and your life.
I won't be here much longer.
In memory of me,
please don't do drugs to numb the pain.
Trust me,
drugs aren't worth it at all.
They will destroy you and your life even more.
If you do start for whatever reason,
please,
find the strength within you to stop.
Too many Indigenous youth die from drugs.
Don't let yourself become one of them.
And don't talk to men online and get into a car
with them.
You'll never be seen again,
and no one will look for you.

I'm sorry,
but it's the truth."
    "Clara,
did Annie die from a drug overdose?
Why would I want to do drugs?"
    "Yes,
she did.
People do drugs for many different reasons."
    "Yeah,
but why would I want to?"
    "To numb the pain!"
she said,
close to tears.
    "Numb the pain?
What pain would I want to numb,
Clara?"
    "The intergenerational trauma;
it is passed down from one generation to the next
generation.
It's a ripple effect.
You see?
If you don't feel the pain from the past,
you'll feel it very soon,
very soon.
Get ready."
I sit in silence...
This pain Clara spoke of was new to me,
but somehow I knew it was part of my family and
my people.

"Are you addicted to drugs,
Clara?
Were you?"
She sat there just staring at me.
She has a very sad look in her eyes.
I sat there silently,
feeling very sick to my stomach.
Something terrible is about to happen.
We hugged for a very long time.
She left the next day before I woke up.
I never saw her again,
but I promised never to forget her.
Promises are promises, and promises are unbreakable.

The Hand ☾ Jane Nocona
July 27, 2021
In an alleyway

She was right.
Of course she was!
Clara was one of the smartest and toughest
people I know.

You can run,
but you can't hide.

Since she left,
I find myself peeking
around
buildings,
hallways,
anywhere,
everywhere.
My surroundings.
Running
from
the

blood.

Red.

Hand.

The Bloody Red Hand ☾ *Jane Nocona*

It is always on me.
It covers my mouth.
It keeps me silent–
from speaking out...
It makes me paranoid.
I can't breathe with it.
I have gotten used to it.
I wish I hadn't.
The bloody red hand is probably
invisible to you.
If you cared enough to look closer
and deeper,
you would probably see it.

Who am I ☾ Jane Nocona

Oh yes...
An introduction...
I forgot to introduce myself,
didn't I?
My name is Jane.
I gave myself the name *Nocona* for a
last name because it means *wanderer*.
I am a wanderer.
I am an Indigenous teen girl from
Nebraska.
I have been living in the foster care
system in Omaha for the past sixteen
years.
My favorite subjects are Science and
English.
I have gone to many schools and lived
with many families...
some better others.

Moon ☾ Jane Nocona

I am lying on my bed
staring up at
the ceiling.
I try to close my eyes,
but when I do,
tears sting my eyes.
I look over at the moon and
remember what my mom
always said at the end of each
story...
The moon sees me,
the moon sees you.
I love when Coyote
comes out every night to see Moon
and to sing to her.
It reminds me that somewhere,
someone is looking at the same
moon.

Phases of the Moon ☾ *Jane Nocona*

I like to think of the *faces* of the moon,
because the moon looks like she has a
face,
or many of them I should say.
Here's a list I wrote for you in my diary.
New Moon–
New Beginnings.
Waxing Crescent Moon–
Light.
First Quarter Moon
(Half Moon)–
Commitment of Action.
Waxing Gibbous–
Developmental Stage.
Full Moon–
The Physical and Emotional Body.
Waning Gibbous–
Get rid of negative thoughts.
There are many more...
these are just a few.

Constellations ☾ Jane Nocona

The stars and planets are so
intriguing.
Each constellation has its own
meaning and individualism...
like people.
When I gaze up at the stars, I see
the constellations...

URSA MAJOR: *THE GREAT BEAR.*
CASSIOPEIA: *THE SEATED QUEEN.*
ORION: *THE HUNTER.*
CANIS MAJOR: *THE GREATER DOG.*
CENTAURUS: *THE CENTUR.*
CRUX: *THE SOUTHERN CROSS.*

No one has really paid attention to-
Ophiuchus.
The Serpent Bearer.
It's shaped like a man holding a serpent.
I've only seen it once.
That *night...*
I'll never forget it.

Indigenous Myths
and Legends ☾ Jane Nocona

are what keep me connected to my
ancestors and what keep my hopes
alive.
I don't know if I'm Lakota;
I read the myths and legends.
They are comforting and
connecting:
Malina- Sun Goddess in Inuit,
Ix Chel - Mayan Moon Goddess,
How Rabbit Caught Sun in a Trap,
Thunderbird,
Coyote and Moon,
Devil's Tower,
and
The Lost Trail of Colorado.

Dark Side of the Moon ☾ *Jane Nocona*

The dark side of the moon and I are alike.
We are both mysterious and unreadable.
The holes in the moon and the holes in my
heart are secrets.
They are hidden in the deep,
dark, vast emptiness of the cosmos.
They are secrets that no one will ever know.
The moon and I,
as you can see,
we are very much alike.

4

NUMB

A MEMORY

☾

At first,
it hurts a little,
I remember,
but once it's done I don't feel anything.
Then,
I don't feel any pain...
Not from the intergenerational trauma or
from what has personally happened to me
in my life.
I am now numb.
Totally numb.
So numb it's a little scary.
I lean back against the wall in my room.
My body begins to feel heavy...
especially my arms and legs.
Then the nausea washes over me; I
feel very sick.
I rush over to the desk and grab a
trash bin.
After I throw up I sit down.
I slump my head down onto the chair facing my
desk.
My mouth begins to feel dry.
Water.
I think to myself.
I need to get water.
I must get water.
I try to get up.
I can't.

My whole body falls into a deep sleep

Clara,

Where Are You? ☾ Jane Nocona

I have no idea...
We lost contact with each other years
ago.
But I still care about her because I still
see her as a really good,
trusting friend.
It was on this day,
July 28th,
that Clara 'left.'
It's been five years since Clara went away.
She was eighteen, and I was twelve.
She was considered "legally" an
adult.
I was considered "legally" a child,
still.
I am now seventeen.
Thirteen was when things went bad.
I hated being a child.
I wish I could've gone out with her.
I wouldn't be so lonely here in this shelter
if the staff members or if Clara allowed me
to go.
I can imagine her claiming that it would be
too dangerous and that the streets are no

place for a little girl.
Trust me,
I was twelve.
I wasn't a baby.
I always wonder what happened to her.
The thoughts and scenarios I make up in my
head haunt me constantly.
I hate seeing what people go through here in
this shelter;
it breaks my heart.
I stomp up the stairs to my bedroom with my
fists balled.
My long fingernails feel as if they might pierce
my skin.
I feel as if I might cry.
I'm scared.
I'm angry.
I'm heartbroken.
I beat myself up over the fact that I broke one
of many promises I made to Clara.
I'm scared of what I'm going through.
I'm angry at the things I'm going through.
I'm heartbroken because of what I'm going
through.
I'm angry at what happened to Clara.
                              I'm angry at what *could've*
                              happened to her.
I'm angry at what is happening to me.

ONE YEAR LATER...

2022

☾

The Little Pink Box ☾ Jane Nocona
January 2, 2022
Drew's Drug Store
Omaha, Nebraska

Some of the other girls who I live with at the
shelter are standing outside at Drew's Drug
Store.
My hair blows a little in the wind.
I brush the tangled strands away from my face.
I take a deep breath,
open the door,
and walk in.
Lydia holds the door open for me and smiles.
I smile back at her.
    "Thank you,
Lydia."
    "You're welcome,
Jane,"
she says,
shutting the door behind us.
As the girls look at the eyeshadow and lip
gloss,
I drift to another aisle.
I pick up the little pink box.
How am I going to get the thing?
Should I hide it in my sweatshirt?

No,
shoplifting will get me in trouble.
I will carry it to the other register and hope that
Lydia and the other girls don't notice.

"Jane,"
Julia calls as she waves at me.
I look up.

"Lydia said that it's time to go back now,"
Julia says.
She looks at me.
Up.
Down.
It makes me uncomfortable.

"Are you okay?"
she asks,
smiling a little.

"Yeah."
Did she see it?
The little pink box?

The first Test I
Hope to Fail ☾ Jane Nocona

After we get home,
I head off to the restroom next to my room.
In the bathroom,
I have a toilet,
a sink,
and a tiny
shower.
When I'm done my heart sinks.
My hands are quivering as I stare
at the test.
Tears cloud my eyes.
I gasp.
My whole body begins to shake and
go numb.
Two thin blue lines.
One if I am *not* pregnant.
Two *if I am.*
I can't be pregnant.
I can't be pregnant.
But I am.
I am six weeks pregnant.
What am I going to do now?

In the Common Area
at the Shelter ☾ Jane Nocona

It's after hours,
and I walk into the common area.
I never get caught.
Never.
The thrill of being ignored.
Unseen.
I wrap a light pink blanket around my
shoulders.
My earbuds are in.
I am in front of the screen and the rest
of the world is gone.
The illumination is glaring into my face.
It burns.
Just like the truth.

Later That Night ☾ *Jane Nocona*

I hate what I see on the screen.
I read it in a whisper...
I tighten my lips and punch the computer
with all of my strength.
It falls off the table and hits the
floor with a loud thud.
I watch the screen shatter.
It shattered the same way I shattered.
Crashed.
Cracked.
Shattered.
I get up.
The blanket falls from my shoulders.
The earbuds fall and the plug comes
loose from my outdated phone.
The music plays loud,
very loud.
It is so loud that I fear that the guitar rifts
will wake up the whole shelter!
The rest of the world
is back,
and

I
had
enough.

"I'M DONE!
I'M REALLY DONE!
I'M GOING TO QUIT!"
This time I am actually going to quit...
for real.
I need to save the life within me while I still can.
I throw my hands up into the air.
"CLARA IS GOING TO BE SO PROUD
OF ME!"
I run around the room,
grab my bag,
and leave the shelter

quietly
like
a
mouse.

No one hears.
No one sees.
I walk a few miles
and stop at the river.
I stand on the bridge.
My hair is blowing.
Out of the middle of nowhere I cry.
I take out one pill
and

throw it into the river
screaming,
"THAT ONE IS FOR MY MOTHER!
I reach in for another.
"THAT ONE IS FOR CLARA!"
I lean against the railing.
I try to catch my breath.
But instead,
I cry so hard that I feel like I could choke.
Then another surge of anger goes through me
and I scream,
"THIS ONE IS FOR MY
CHILD!"
I throw another one over the bridge.
And another.
"THIS ONE IS FOR ME!"
I am out of breath.
I stand there.
I make a promise to myself that I would
Never
touch
those pills again.
Never.
I can't let them hurt me anymore.
I can't,
and I won't.
Never.

I Stand There ☾ *Jane Nocona*
That Bridge in Omaha

I stare
down
into the abyss of dark water beneath
the bridge.
My arms and chest feel pinned to the
black metallic railing.
The railing is cold and wet;
it was raining a little before and only
drizzling now.
I look at my hands.
They're shaking.
They're cold.
They're turning shades of blue and
purple.
My long nails are piercing my hands
causing droplets of blood.
I rub them onto my thin black jacket.
I sniffle and wipe another tear from
my eye and run my hand through my
damp hair.
I stare
up
at the cold and dreary Omaha sky.
I've never felt this empowered before.

I've never felt so uncertain before.
I think of something Clara said to me
that I'll never forget.
She said,
    "Jane,
no one else here has hope,
not even me,
but you do.
There's still time for you."
Why me?
What's so special about me?
I feel like crying.
I feel like screaming-
again.
But I remain silent.

Blackbird ☾ *Jane Nocona*

Back at my room,
I lie in bed,
wide awake.
I am thinking about the *life*
inside of me.
I am thinking about the lives
I miss...
Out of the window,
I see the blackbird who visits me.
    "Hi,
I say.
Blackbird visits from time-
to-
time.
She seems like she can hear
me.
She looks back at me.
    "I *see* you,"
I say,
looking into her beautiful eyes.
    "Do you see me?"
She just looks at me and tilts her
head a little.
I remember Clara loved birds and the

moon.
She had a certain
fondness for blackbirds.

    "Tell Clara that I love her,
and I miss her."
I look up at the moon.
    "H-
hi Clara,
wherever you are,"
I say with my voice shaking.

                    Blackbird flies away...

The moon sees you.

The moon sees me.

Asking For Help ☾ *Jane Nocona*
January 31, 2022

I stand in the doorway to Lydia's office
like I always do when I need her.
I need her more than ever now.
I'm waiting for her to finish talking with
someone.
I think she's in a meeting or something.
A man walks out.
I peek in.
   "Come in,"
she says,
gesturing me to come in.
   "Sit down."
She motions to the chair.
I sit down.
She leans forward and asks,
   "How are you doing,
Jane?"
      "I have something to tell you."
      "Yes?"
      "I-
I hope you won't be mad at me."
   "Why?
Why would I be mad at you?"
      "I-

I am pr-

pre-

pregnant."

    "Oh,

Jane.

Why would I be mad at you?

I'll help you."

    "What's going to happen to me now?"

    "We will get you help."

I nod my head.

    "Th-

thank you."

It's a Girl! ☾ *Jane Nocona*
February 10, 2022

I am at the women's health center.
Lydia drove me.
It's been a long time since I left the
facility. I've been clean for a good
while now.
  "Do you want to know the
gender of your child?"
I look at Lydia and,
I look at the doctor.
  "It's your choice,
Jane."
I look back at the doctor and nod my
head.
  "Congratulations,
Jane!
It's a girl!"
It's a girl!
Is a phrase that I will always remember
and cherish for the rest of my life.
Tears of joy fall down my cheeks.
I gaze up at the monitor.
  "She's so little!"
  "She is!
She's tiny!"

"Just like me.

Is she sucking her thumb?"

The doctor looks closer at the screen.

"She is!"

she says,

smiling.

We laugh together.

This is the first time I've smiled and laughed

in a very long time.

Today is a day of hope...

one of the happiest days of my life!

The Birth of Hazel ☾ Jane Nocona
April 13, 2022
Omaha, Nebraska

After the birth of Hazel,
I feel an intense responsibility caring for
and protecting this tiny and precious little
life.
    "Here she is,
Jane."
A smiling midwife says,
handing Hazel over to me.
She is wrapped in a bundle of fluffy and soft
blankets.
My first thought when I see her is...
My God...
She's beautiful and tiny.
She looks like a mini-
me.
I know that I will love her forever.
I think to myself,
What am I going to do now?
I am a teen mom.
    "I love you,
Hazel,
I will take care of you."

Phone Call ☾ Lydia Fox
May 1st, 2022
Omaha Foster Care Center
Omaha, Nebraska

I am calling a family in Custer,
South Dakota to see if they will
foster Jane and Hazel for a little
while.
The phone rings.
    "Henderson residence."
    "Hello,
Sarah,
this is Lydia Fox from Omaha Foster
Care Center."
    "Oh!
Hello again,
Lydia!
How have you been?"
    "I've been good.
How about you and your family?"
    "Oh,
we're fine.
Rachel is excited about school."
    "I do have a young lady who will
be eighteen next year."
    "My family and I would absolutely

love to take her in."

"I must add that she has a newborn
baby girl.
This is much more than taking in a teen..."
There is silence.

"My family will take good care of
them.
I feel this is something we must do.
What are their names?"

"Jane and Hazel."

5

Pack Your Bags ☾ *Jane Nocona*
May 3rd, 2022
Foster Care Center Office
Omaha, Nebraska

I knock on Jane's door.
    "Hey,
Jane,
may I speak to you for a moment?"
    "Yeah,
one second."
She opens the door.
    "Hi?"
    "I found a foster family for you
and Hazel."
She begins scrambling in her room
grabbing stuff and throwing it all into

two big duffle bags.

"Do you want me to help you pack?"

"Sure."

"When are we going?
And where are we going?"

"You're going to Custer,
South Dakota...
tomorrow.
They're a good family,
Jane."

I nod agreeingly.

"I trust you."

"I know you do,
and I want you to know that I value your
trust."

"I know."

I smile anxiously at her.

"Thank you for everything,
Lydia.
I really appreciate you.
We both do."

The Long
Road to Custer ☾ Jane Nocona
May 4, 2022

I stare out the window and hold Hazel's
tiny hand during the car ride to Custer.
The world goes by,
and I watch.
Lydia looks over her shoulder at Hazel
and me.
She smiles.
 "How's Hazel doing?"
 "She's good,
she sleeps a lot."
 "That's what babies do."
 "Yeah,
but she keeps me very busy...
in a good way."
We sit silently for a little while...
 "I quit for Hazel,
you know."
 "I know you did.
You quit for yourself too.
You quit because you didn't want it to
destroy your life."
I almost want to laugh.
I don't.

There's a lot I haven't told her and I doubt
I ever will,
not because I don't trust her.
Some conversations just never happen,
not because I don't want to tell her,
but because the time is never the right
time.

Two Little Teddy Bears ☾ Jane Nocona
May 4th, 2022

We get out of the car.
Lydia helps me with Hazel.
There's a family of three smiling at
us:
A girl with strawberry blonde hair
who
looks a little younger than me and
a mom and dad.
      "Welcome,
Jane.
Welcome,
Hazel,"
the parents say.
    "Thank you,"
I say as I smile at them.
The girl walks up to me.
    "I can help you carry your stuff
in and show you your room."
    "Okay,
thank you."
    "My name is Rachel by the way,
Rachel Henderson."
    "Nice to meet you,"
she says,

holding the door open for me while I carry
Hazel.
"Thank you,
Rachel.
And nice to meet you too."
"Yep,
you're welcome."
I follow her up a wooden,
spiral staircase.
I look all around me.
"Nice house you have here."
"Thanks,
I'll tell my grandpa that my new friends,
Jane and Hazel,
like it.
He designed it and helped build it."
"Oh,
wow,
that's super cool,
Rachel."
She nods her head and brings Hazel and me
to a white door.
"Welcome
to your new room,"
she says,
opening the door.
My eyes widen.
"This is beautiful."
"Glad you like it.

I got you and Hazel something!"
She runs out.
I put Hazel in the crib and give her a toy.
She starts chewing on it like a puppy.
A few minutes later,
Rachel is back carrying two teddy bear dolls:
Both with big, happy smiles and yellow bows.
    "This is going to sound a bit weird and
childish to you...
We went out the day after we learned we
were going to take care of you and Hazel and
got these corny little teddy bears because
we care about you and Hazel."
    "Aww,
thank you!
That's the sweetest thing ever.
    "Thank you."
    "You are welcome."

You Learn to Live
With Memories ☾ Jane Nocona

I unpack and get settled after the long
ride from Omaha to Custer.
Hazel looks at the new room,
and I take a deep breath,
The small clock on the
nightstand says
5:55.
Hazel and I arrived here ten minutes ago,
but it seems like hours...
I have a good feeling about Rachel and her
family.
Tired, I lie down on the bed
and open my diary and write-
I think that Hazel and I will like this place.
I think we'll be alright.
I almost fell asleep,
but the memories keep me awake.
I have a lot of memories,
some good,
some bad,
some in between.
Throughout my life I've learned to live
with those memories.
I try to recall the good ones as much as

possible so that I can remember why
I wake up in the morning.
The bad ones...
well,
one should not keep them all bottled up
inside.
The past,
the memories,
and everything in the murky middle
make
you
who
you
are.

The Welcome Dinner ☾ *Jane Nocona*

A little while later,
I come back down the stairs.
    "Jane,"
Rachel's mother calls.
    "Yeah?"
I reply.
    "Come down,
hon."
I come into view.
    "So,
Jane,
as a little welcome,
we would like to take you out to dinner.
What is your favorite food?"
I shrug my shoulders.
    "I don't have any favorite foods,
to be honest.
Whatever you or Rachel want to have is fine."
    "There's a restaurant nearby that we
enjoy,
but it's up to you.
You are our guest,"
the mother says,
smiling.
        "Okay,

we can try that place."
The mother smiles.
    "Let's get in the car girls."
    "Okay!"
Rachel and I walk to the car with Hazel in tow
of course.
She opens the truck door from the
inside.
    "Oh my gosh,
I love Hazel,
she's so cute!"
    "She is,
but she is a lot of work!"
We sit quietly for a little while.
    "What restaurant are we going to?"
    "Bluebell,
it's in the park."
    "Oh cool,"
I say,
nodding.
    "Do you and your family go there a
lot?"
    "No,"
she says,
shaking her head.
    "Only when it's a special occasion."
    "What do you usually get?"
    "Buffalo Meatloaf with mashed potatoes
and cowboy beans.

It's a sin not to get it!
And don't forget root beer!"

Our food and drinks come to our table.
Rachel got Buffalo Meatloaf with mashed
potatoes and cowboy beans.
Sarah got a Ceasar Salad,
but without the croutons
(she's gluten-
free,
whatever that means).
She ordered Raymond a Ribeye Steak.
I got myself meatloaf like Rachel.
        "Raymond will be here soon,
girls."
After a few minutes,
she checks her phone again.
        "He's out in the parking lot,"
she says,
smiling.
I notice her pearly white teeth,
when a police officer walks in.
My blood goes cold,
and my eyes widen.
I feel like the world is frozen
in time.
I
can't
bring
myself
back
into

reality.

    "Hello there,

Jane."

He smiles and sits down next to Sarah.

    "Oh,

hello."

I jerk myself awake.

    "How was the drive?"

    "Good,

but long,"

I say

trying to sound cheerful-not like

seeing a police officer just scared me half to

death.

Arts and Crafts ☾ *Jane Nocona*

"Pss,
Jane."
"Yeah?"
I say,
coming to open the bedroom door.
"Would you like to do some crafts?"
"Sure!
I just put Hazel to bed though,
could we do them downstairs
so she doesn't wake up?"
"Yeah,
that's fine.
Come with me."
We go downstairs.
"What crafts do you like to do?"
I ask.
"I like Origami and making things with
Washi Tape,"
Rachel replies.
"Cool."
She sets the box down and sits.
I sit in front of her.
We are in the living room on a sheepskin rug.
"Well,
what do you enjoy doing?"

"I enjoy reading and writing when I have
time.
I try to write in a diary before I go to bed
and sometimes when I wake up in the morning.
But since I am busy with Hazel,
I write less than I used to."

"That's ok,
Hazel is worth it."
I smile.

"Thanks;
she's my pride and joy."

"Aw..."
She begins folding paper and hands me a piece.

"Thank you...
We work for a while,
until we both decide to call it a night.

The Rules ☾ Jane Nocona
May 5th, 2022

"Hey,
Jane,
Sarah and I thought this
would be a good time to go over the
rules in this household."
I nod my head.
We sit down at the dinner table in
the kitchen.
        "We do not allow
drugs,
alcohol,
or tobacco in or
around our home.
They aren't worth it."
I know, I thought. I know...

Shopping ☾ *Jane Nocona*
May 10th, 2022
Target
Rapid City, South Dakota

"We will buy school things...
Don't worry Jane,
it's is on me."
I nod.
    "Is there anything that we should
get for Hazel?"
    "No,"
I say,
quietly.
    "Sorry,
I didn't hear you,
Hun,"
Rachel's mother says.
    "You don't have to get anything for
Hazel or for me,"
I say,
quietly,
looking down.
I do not want us to take any more from them than
we already are.
    "Hun,

look at me,

I want to do it.

I am doing it for Rachel too.

While you are with us,

I see you as my own child,

and I see Hazel as

my own too."

"Yeah...

Your daughter doesn't have a daughter."

She looks at me sadly.

"Okay,

fine,

you win,"

I say.

She smiles warmly at me.

"Hey,

Jane!

Janie!

I look over with Hazel in my arms.

"Come here!

I found something cute for Hazel!"

I walk over.

"I am going to buy Hazel this."

She holds up the cutest little shirt that's white

with little yellow ducklings all over it.

"Rachel,

that's really thoughtful of you but-."

"Jane,

I am buying it for Hazel because I want you and

Hazel to feel welcome."

Replacement For Clara? ☾ Jane Nocona
May 12, 2022

The thing is,
there's no one quite like Clara.
After I wake up,
I don't get dressed,
I am still wearing a white t-
shirt and
black sweatpants.
Bare-footed, I go and check on Hazel.
She is kicking and crying.
    "Oh,
Hazel,
shhhh,
please be quiet.
You'll wake people up.
You're okay,"
I say,
bending over and lifting her up.
I walk over to the bed and sit down with her in
my arms.
    "Are you hungry,
little Hazelnut?"
I ask,
lifting my night shirt up to nurse her.
She nurses and begins to calm down.

My head slumps down.
I wake myself up and look at the dark ceiling,
then at the alarm clock.
11:45.
Hazel always wakes up at this time.
She stops nursing.
I pull her out from under my shirt and cradle her
in my arms.
I gaze down at her.
She opens her eyes and makes little noises.
I suddenly feel tears coming from my eyes.
She squeezes my hand,
and we fall asleep.
Early in the morning,
I hear movement downstairs.
I leave Hazel sleeping and go down the steps.
    "Jane,"
Sarah calls.
I look up at Sarah from the doorway.
    "I talked to Rachel to see if she would
take you out for a cup of coffee.
She said she would be delighted to.
After her soccer practice,
I'll take you ladies to a coffeehouse
so you can get to know one another."
    "Okay.
That sounds like fun!
Thank you!"
I open the refrigerator and take out a carton

that says chai latte.

"This drink looks good,"
I say.

"Have you ever had a chai before!?"
Rachel asks.

"No,
is it good?"

"Oh yeah!"

"Do you want me to show you how to make
one?"

"Sure,
if it's no trouble."

"No trouble at all,
Janie,
no trouble at all!
I love making people chais!
Are you okay with me calling you,
Janie?"

"Sure."
We start laughing again.

"This is how you make a perfect iced chai
latte.
First,
you place ice into the glass.
Then,
you pour both the milk and the chai drink
into a separate glass.
AND...
SHAKE IT ALL UP!!"

Chai flies everywhere.
We laugh.
    "Oops.
I need to clean that up now."
I walk over and get a towel to help her.
Her mother rolls her eyes and lets out a little
chuckle.
    "What are the other kinds of chai?"
    "Well,
there's Masala chai,
bubble tea chai,
and there are other ones that I can't think of
at the top of my head,
though."
    "Cool."
I nod my head and take a sip.
    "What's in a chai?"
    "cinnamon,
black tea,
and milk.
Sometimes other things,
like sugar."
Chai made me happy.
It won't keep me up all night, and
I can't overdose on it; it can't kill me.
Making a chai latte felt...
What's the word again?
Normal?
Yes,

normal.
Normal.
I have to say,
it felt good.
It feels good to feel normal.

Soccer Practice ☾ Jane Nocona
May 12, 2022
Rapid City, South Dakota

I get into Sarah's car with Rachel.
　"Thank you."
　"You're welcome,
Janie."
She exhales
climbing into the seat beside me
and puts the seatbelt on.
　"How long have you been playing
soccer?"
　"Since I was seven.
I'll be fourteen in a few months."
　"Oh cool!
When's your birthday?"
　"October 31,
2007."
　"You're a Halloween Baby.
When is your birthday?"
　"I was born on January 12,
2005."
　"I want to get you something!
Maybe I could get you a late birthday
gift?"
　"Rachel,

that's awfully sweet of you,
but there's no need."
   "When is Hazel's?"
   "April 13th,
2022."
Rachel tips her head towards the ceiling.
   "Shoot."
   "Really,
it's fine.
I'm just thankful that you and your
family care about Hazel and me.
To me,
that's the best gift I could ever have."
I pat her on the shoulder.
      "What other hobbies do you have?"
      "Cheerleading.
What about you,
Janie?"
I point at Hazel who is playing with her
teddy bear that Sarah got for her.
      "Hazel,
she's my hobby.
She is my everything."
I was thinking to myself...
she is also a *distraction.*

Distraction ☾ **Jane Nocona**

I learned I was pregnant early.
I was motivated.
If I learned later...
Later would've been too late.
Way too late.
I've been clean for almost a year
now.
There's always the possibility one
could
relapse.

6

At the Field ☾ *Jane Nocona*
May 12, 2022
Rapid City, South Dakota

"See ya,
Rachel.
Have fun."
    "I will,
see ya,
Jane,
see ya,
Hazel,
see ya,
mom."
Sarah and I get some of our stuff from the
car and walk over to the soccer
field.
 We sit down in the stadium.

"Would you like some water,
Jane?"
"Please,
thank you."
Sarah digs in a tote-
bag she brought and pulls out a plastic water
bottle.
She hands it to me.
"Thank you,
Sarah."
"You're welcome,
Jane."
I open it and take a sip.
"Does Hazel want something?"
"She probably wants her bottle.
I'm going to go take her to the restroom now."
I get up and take Hazel to the restroom to
change her.
After approximately fifteen minutes,
I come back and sit back down next to Sarah.
We watch Rachel play soccer with her friends.
"Wow,
she's really good!"
"Oh yes,"
Sarah nods her head,
smiling.
"And she enjoys it very much."
I take out my phone and videotape her playing.
Then out of the middle of nowhere...

Bluebird Coffee Co. ☾ Jane Nocona
May 12, 2022
Rapid City, South Dakota

I look over at Rachel.
 "Are you okay?
Your shoulder was hit pretty hard!"
 "I'm okay,"
she smiles.
 "Mom,
what coffeehouse are we going to?"
 "The Bluebird in Rapid City."
 "Thanks,
mom."
 "Wait,
isn't there another Bluebird Coffee Co.
in Custer right by the house too?"
 "It's a franchise."
 "Oh,
okay."
 "Which location do you like better?"
 "Rapid City.
The drinks just taste better."
 A few minutes later,
Sarah drops us off at the coffeehouse,
and
Rachel goes in first while I get situated

with Hazel.

We follow Rachel inside.

Back to School ☾ *Jane Nocona*
August 15, 2022

It is the first day of school and the first day
of daycare for Hazel.
She goes to the high school daycare,
while I try to finish my senior year.
After school I walk home.
I have a backpack strapped to my back
and Hazel pinned to my chest.
Lydia gave me the backpack and strap
carrier when she left me with the
Hendersons.
Grateful....

Coffee With Rachel ☾ Jane Nocona
August 20, 2022
Bluebird Coffeehouse

It's nice inside.
Nice... like nothing bad would happen here.
I look down at Hazel and kiss her forehead.
My long hair falls onto her face;
she sneezes.
I wipe her nose.
    "Do you like it here,
Hazelnut?
Huh?"
I bounce her around a little to help her sleep.
    "Rachel is going to be here soon."
I look over and see a redheaded girl walking in.
    "Hey,
Rachel."
I stand up and wave in her direction.
She looks up and waves back.
She walks over,
smiling.
    "Hi,
Jane."
    "I hope this is a good location for us
to meet today."
    "This is perfect!"

"I just thought that it would be nice if we
just get some girl time."

"This is going to be fun!"

"What do you want?."

We look up at the menu.

"Hungry?

Thirsty? "

"I don't know...

What do you usually get here?"

"Ummm."

She looks up at the board too.

"Usually,

I get the Honey Badger and a Baguette."

"Ooo,

those sound good,

they sound really good!

What's a Honey Badger?"

"The Honey Badger is suuuuuuuper good!

Jane,

it's the best chai I've ever had!

Seriously!"

"Oh yeah?!

What's in it?"

"Coconut,

Almond,

or dairy milk.

Cinnamon,

and honey.

The honey and cinnamon are what make it

even better.

Oh yeah...

and caffeine,

lot's and lot's of caffeine!"

We laugh.

After we order,

we sit at a booth near the window

overlooking the vast wilderness of the Black Hills.

"Jane,"

Rachel says,

looking up at me.

She is covering her mouth because

she is eating a baguette.

"Can I get a seat for Hazel?

Your arms must be getting tired."

"It's fine,

but thank you."

"You are welcome."

She sits back down.

"So,

how's school going?"

"Pretty good."

"I bet it's tough being the *new kid*."

"Yeah,

I'm used to it

though."

"Do you have any tests or whatnot coming up?

Are people kind to you?"

"Yeah,

I have a science test coming up."
　　"What science class do you take?"
　　"Chemistry...
what science class do you take?"
　　"I am in biology.
What's your favorite class?"
　　"Chemistry and English.
I'm a weird human being,"
I say,
holding a small piece of the baguette up to my
mouth.
We laugh.
　　"No,
Jane,
you're not."
　　"Yes,
I am."
　　"Haha,
but you're my kind of weird."
We eat quietly for a little while.
　　"Thank you again,
Rachel.
This Honey Badger is really good!
You can really taste the honey and cinnamon!
　Love that!"

Fall

☽

Football Game ☾ *Jane Nocona*
September 9, 2022
Custer Cougars Football Field
7 pm

"Hey,
Jane,"
Allie calls,
tying her hair into a messy do.
"My hair is so-
gah!"
she says,
throwing her hands down.
"It's a hot mess in the back,
but I don't care."
Allie and I laugh.
"Where's Hazel?
Is she okay?"
she asks.
"She's okay,
she's with Rachel's mom.
Mrs. Henderson wants me to 'socialize' with
my 'peers.'
She wants me to feel normal
sometimes,"
I say.
I then realize Allie probably doesn't understand.

I wonder why I say these things especially to
Allie.
     "Where's Valerie and Vivian?"
she responds.
I shrug my shoulders.
     "They should be here soon,"
she says.
     "Okay,
do you want to sit down or do you want to get
something to drink or eat first?"
     "I don't care,"
I say.
     "Let's get settled before it all fills up."
I nod.
We go and sit down close to the front and near
the pep band.
     "I don't mean to sound critical,
Allie,
but why are the boys wearing those stupid teeny
tiny pants?"
She laughs.
     "You're funny...
     "I don't know,"
she says.
     "Well,
they look stupid,"
I say.
We laugh.
     "They do!"

"But they do look kind of cute."

I laugh too.

But not like Allie.

After we get our drinks,
we go back to our seats and read the roster for the
Custer Cougars.
Joseph Calls His Horses
Freshman 5'11" 300 lb #77
James Alden
Freshman 5'2" 200 lb #18
Jacob Ansley
Freshman 6'3" 400 lb #1
Liam Baldwin
Freshman 5'7" 450 lb #16
Michael Cage
Sophomore 5'7" 238 lb #9
Karter Cuskar
Senior 6'3" 245 lb #27
River Custer
Sophomore 6'1" 300 lb #10
Harrison John Davis
Senior 5'11" 150 lb #67
Tadd Jerkins
Junior 5'11" 250 lb #86
Todd Zigger
Senior 5'10" 160 lb #78
Haydn Zimmerman
Senior 6'9" 250 lb #89

And there's many more.

After the Football Game ☾ Jane Nocona
September 9, 2022
Custer Cougars Football Field
11 pm

The stadium lights are still illuminating the field.
    "Well,
it was fun hanging out with you,"
Allie says.
        "You as well,
Allie."
We get up and share a polite hug.
        "Hey,
Jane,
how about we hang out again sometime,
you can bring Hazel."
Allie leaves me to go with her older sister who
picks her up.
I stand there with one arm around the metal fence
surrounding the field and the stadium.
I look at my phone,
scroll through my social media, and then look up
because I sense something terrible is about to
happen.
My heart starts beating fast.
It gets faster and faster.
BUMP!

"Oh,
I'm sorry!
Didn't mean to do that."
"Oof.
You're good."
Then I wait.
What was I waiting for?
The hand to touch me...
again?
I look at him funny.
He looks back at me funny,
too.
"Are you okay?
Did I scare you?"
I stand there speechless.
I stand there stunned.
I am wild-
eyed.
"N-
I'm fine."
I turn around and walk away,
but look back at him.
He has a worried look in his eyes.
I nod.
"I am,
I am fine."
He stays far back from me and then moves closer.
He looks at me sadly.
"It's me,

Harrison,
it's okay now.
I won't hurt you."
I think about how skittish I am around boys.
I really don't trust them,
but I want to be "normal."

Big Sister Figure ☾ Rachel Henderson
September 10, 2022
Sitting on top of a hill
Mid afternoon, Custer State Park

After Jane and I get into the kitchen I say,
  "You know,
Jane?"
  "Yes?"
she says,
looking at me.
  "I always wanted a big sister."
Jane nods.
  "You are the closest thing I have to a big
sister.
I know you are not my *biological sister.*
But you are the best big sister figure someone
could ever ask for."
Jane smiles.
  "Aw,
Rachel,
that's the nicest thing someone has ever said
to me!"
  "Well,
 it's the truth,
Jane."
Jane grins and says,

"That's really sweet of you,
Rachel.
You are one of the best friends I've ever had."
Jane hugs me,
and I hug her back.

What Do You Want to Do After You Graduate? ☾ Jane Nocona

It sort of catches me off guard when the
school counselor asks.
I tell her that after I graduate I want help
people.
I want to help young people who are
fighting
drug addiction,
and I want to help the Indigenous women
and girls who are at risk.
She smiles and nods her head.
    "I think that would be wonderful.
You could save a lot of lives."
I look at her and try to smile,
but the smile is in a sad sort of way.
I feel like I might cry.
She probably senses that I am feeling kind
of sad.
Truth is,
I feel guilty there were a lot of times when
I was out on the streets when I shouldn't have
been,
I should have died.
I don't deserve to be alive and I don't deserve
the people I have met so far at the school.

"Oh,

Jane,"

she says looking at me and then making a grab
for the tissue box.

I am so deep in thought I don't even realize that
I am crying.

"Here you go,"

she says,

handing me some tissues.

"Thank you.'

She leans forward a little.

"Jane,

what are you thinking about hun?"

"Na-

no,

it's fine.

Something just made me feel really sad."

"Do you want to talk about it?"

"It's too personal.

It's just memories from my life before I moved
here.

Sorry,

I just got a little emotional there."

"It's okay Jane,

if you ever want to talk I will listen
to you."

"Oh,

I know."

Book Club ☾ Jane Nocona
September 14, 2022
Henderson Residence

"Rachel,
I know how much you like books and
all of that...
I heard that there's a book club at school
now,
and I thought of you."
A sarcastic and happy grin appears on
her face.
　　"I actually started it."
　　"You did!?"
Rachel asks.
　　"Why weren't you at the
meeting today during 7th period study
hall,"
I ask.
　　"I failed a science test and mom
is going to make me retake it,"
Rachel says,
grimly with her arms crossed against her
chest.
　　"You know I can help you with that.
Science is one of my favorite classes!"
I say.

"You know,

Jane,

I wish I were smart like you,"

Rachel remarks.

"Oh Rachel,

you're smart.

Science is just harder for you.

That dosen't make you stupid or anything like

that.

What science class are you in,

and when are you

planning on retaking it?"

"Biology,

stupid Biology,

stupid,

stupid Biology.

I am retaking it tomorrow.

What book are we reading in Book Club by the

way?"

"We are reading *The Book Thief* by Markus

Zusak,"

I say.

"Ooo,

I like that book!

"Zusak is an amazing writer!

I can help you later tonight after I tuck

Hazel in.

I promise I won't forget,"

I say.

"I know,

Jane,

you never forget."

Study Night ☾ *Jane Nocona*

"I am making some cookies
for our little study session tonight.
What is your favorite cookie?"
Rachel asks.
I put my book down.
"I don't really have a favorite cookie.
What's your favorite cookie?"
"Um,
Snickerdoodles are really good.
Would you like to try that?"
"Sure!"
"Okay!"
Rachel says,
rushing over to the kitchen.
After she puts the cookies in the oven,
I join her in the kitchen.
I grab a large steel
mixing bowl and put it onto the table.
"Rachel,
look at this bowl."
She turns.
"Hazel could probably fit in that
thing."
She laughs.
"Hahaha!

She probably could!
Put her in and see!"
I put a towel in and got Hazel out of her
playpen in the living room and put her gently
in the mixing bowl.
"She fits!"
I say,
looking over my shoulder.
Rachel looks over.
    "Awww,
 I'll take a picture!"
    "Could you send it to me
please?"
    "Of course!"
She pulls out her phone.
    "I think that you just got it."
I pull out my phone.
    "Aww,
thank you so much,
Rachel!
It's so cute!"
    "You're welcome,
Janie."
Rachel says,
beaming.
WHAM!
WHAM!
WHAM!
    "Hazel,

wh-

what are you doing?

You crazy little child?"

    "Oh shoot!

The cookies!"

Rachel grabs an oven mitt and rush down and get the
cookies.

    "They're okay!"

I walk over.

     "Ooooo.

They look good,

Rachel."

We grab plates and glasses of milk and get settled
at the table to study.

    "So,

what part of science is the hardest for you?"

   "Everything."

   "Everything?"

   "Yes,

all of it."

   "What part in biology was the test over?"

    "Errrrrrr,

it was over-

uh-

I will just-

just take-

just look at the study guide,"

Rachel says,

fumbling for the study guide in her backpack.

She takes out the folder and gives it to me.
    "Here ya go."
I flip through the pages.
    "So,
it looks like biology chapter four?
Three to four?"
I ask,
looking up at her.
She nods her head.
    "Okay."
    "Can you please help,
Jane."
    "Oh yes,
of course I can."
    "Wow...
 this study guide is the size of the Bismarck!"
Rachel says.
I laugh.
    "I mean look at the thing,
Janie!"
    "Yeah,
my back hurts just looking at it,
girl."
We laugh.

After School ☾ *Harrison John Davis*
September 15, 2022
Custer Central High

I see Jane at her locker with her backpack and
walk up to talk to her.
"Hey,
Jane."
"Oh,
hi there,
Harrison."
She flips her backpack over her shoulders.
We begin to walk down the hall.
"I was wondering if you would like to hang out
sometime."
"Just to hang out,
not a date thing?"
I nod.
"That sounds good,
I would like that a lot,
Harrison,"
she says
smiling.
I smile back and step closer to her.
"When would it work for you?"
I ask.
"How about Friday after school?"

"I would say yes,
but I have football practice everyday after
school,
unfortunately."
        "Oh,
right.
I knew that!
Huh,
maybe a Saturday afternoon,
sometime?"
        "Don't feel bad.
Saturday would work."
        "I'll give you my phone number."
She pulls out her phone.
        "Oh my!
I need to go get *someone*,
Harrison.
You can come with me,
though."
        "Okay."
I nod and follow her down the hall.
        "I don't want you to be late for
practice though," she says.
        "Don't worry about it."
We get to the nursery in the school.
I am a little confused...
and wonder why Jane is going there.
        "Who are you picking up?"
I ask.

A teacher approaches Jane and says,
     "Oh yes,
Jane,
I'm sorry,
I knew it was you.
     I'll go get Hazel for you."
I squint my eyebrows and am
still confused.
Who is Hazel?
I wonder.
I tap her gently on the shoulder.
     "Jane,
who is Hazel?"
     "S-
she's my d-
daughter,"
she says,
stammering and turning her head to look
at me.
I try not to act surprised,
but I am surprised.
     "Y-
you're a mom?"
     "Yes."
She says,
quietly while nodding her head and looking
away from me.
The same woman who talked to Jane just
minutes earlier comes back with a baby

dressed in an outfit with ducklings on it.
All of the sudden,
I start to feel bad for both of them.
Oh Jane.
She puts on a sling and puts Hazel inside it
and says,
    "Did you have a good day?"
She strokes her daughter's feathery hair.
I stand there speechless wondering how in
the world Jane does it.
    "Hazel,
this is my friend,
Harrison,
he's a senior too,"
she says
sweetly as she continues to stroke her hair.
    "Hey there,
Hazel,"
I say.
She just stares at me,
but she's the sweetest thing.
    "How old is she?"
    "She's six months."
I stare.
    "So,
Harrison,
do you still want my phone number?"
I am silent for a moment...
    "Yes.

Yes I do."

I pull out my phone.

"What's your number?"

"402-445-8967."

"I'll text you."

Saturday Afternoon ☾ Jane Nocona
September 17, 2022
Custer, South Dakota

I get dressed and go to Hennie's Ice Cream
Shop to meet Harrison.
     "I love you,
Hazel,
be good for Rachel and Sarah."
     "She will,
Jane!
You don't have to worry about a thing!"
I put my pack on and walk out.
     "Have fun with Harrison and be safe!"
Sarah calls as I walk out of the door.
I walk over to the ice cream shop and sit down
once I get inside.
I look at my phone and wait for Harrison.
I think it's more polite to wait to order.
     "Hi,
there,
Jane."
I look up to see Harrison.
     "Oh,
hey there,
Harrison."
     "Why didn't you get anything?"

"I was waiting for you."

"Jane,
please,
seriously,
you didn't have to do that."

"No,
no,
it was fine."
We go up and order ice cream.
I get a sorbet called Peachy Mango and
Harrison gets a chocolate peanut butter
one called Dump Truck or Dirt Bike,
something like that.
I like Harrison—
a lot.

HOMECOMING GAME AND DANCE

☾

Homecoming is apparently big deal here in
Custer.
The school colors are blue and white and are
all over the place.
Everyone is going to the game.
I was told that they have the dance outside.
Sarah said she would watch Hazel,
so I guess I am going.
But I am not planning on staying long because
I need to go home to Hazel.
I am not fond of leaving her,
not because I don't trust Sarah...
Don't get me wrong,
she's been nothing
but kind to Hazel and me.
It's because of Hazel,
my little Hazelnut.
She needs me.
And I need her.

7

Would You Like to Dance ☾ Jane Nocona

I am sitting by myself watching Rachel slow-
dancing with Tadd...
    "Hey,"
I hear a familiar voice through the loud music.
I look up.
It's Harrison.
    "Hello,"
I say.
Harrison is tall and strong.
His skin is pale,
and he has shiny,
wavy strawberry blonde hair and
blue-
green
eyes.
I have long black hair,
dark brown eyes,

and darker skin.
In many ways,
we seem different.
I wonder if this matters?
I don't know if I'll ever know.
    "Do you want to dance?"
    "Uh-
Okay-
I would love to.
Thank you."
He holds out his hand to me.
I take his hand,
and he leads me to the center of
the dance floor,
which is a parking space for the buses.
My heart is beating fast.
So fast that I fear that it might jump out.

8

❦

Eighty-Seven Percent ☾ Rachel Henderson
September 22, 2022

My first thought after my biology teacher
hands back the test back is,
I have got to tell Janie about this!
After school,
I walk down the hallway to
find Jane.
She is pulling stuff out of her locker and
talking to people.
    "GUESS WHAT I GOT,
JANE!"
    "A jar of dirt?"
she laughs.
    "I GOT AN Eighty-
seven percent on the retake!"
    "Oh yay!

Good job!"
She gives me a hug.
"Thank you!"
"I knew you could do it,
I am very proud of you,"
she says.
I smile and wrap my arm around her.

The Pickup Truck ☾ Jane Nocona

I am in Rachel's car waiting for her to come
out.
I am sitting in the front seat and looking
out the window.
It is starting to rain.
To my horror,
I see a black pickup truck parked near a
light.
I stare at it for a little while.
Creeeeek.
The door opens,
and I jump into defense mode.
        "Hi,
Jane."
Rachel.
Thank God.
        "Oh,
hey,
Rachel."
We buckle up.
She puts her hands on the steering wheel,
but before she drives away I say,
        "Rachel,
do you know whose truck that is?"

She looks out of the window.
"You mean that one?"
She points.
I nod.
"Oh,
that's Kyler Joseph Mitchel's truck.
He isn't a student here-
oh sh-!
He's coming
Get down,
JANE!"
We get down.
"Wh-
who is he,
Rachel?"
She puts her finger to her lips and her eyes widen.
She looks back up.
"Stay down,
Jane."
She says,
looking back at me.
Her eyes are wide open.

Kyler Joseph Mitchel ☾ *Rachel Henderson*

"Rachel,
who was that guy?"
"Well,
not someone who you want to meet,
Janie.
He-
there have been some women and girls in the area
who have disappeared and no one knows where
they are."
I shudder at the thought.
"But don't worry
Jane,
you and Hazel are completely safe with us.
I would *never ever* let something horrible happen
to you or Hazel.
We love you too much.
You never have to fear while you live with us."
She goes up to bed.
I am still pretty shaken up.
I look up at the TV that is still playing in the living
room.
News Anchor: Two girls from Spearfish,
South Dakota are missing:
Allie Erics is fifteen and Kali Johns is thirteen.

Please keep a look out for them.
I stare at the tv.
I hear Hazel crying.
I go up to help her go back to sleep.
I don't want her to wake others up.
After I tuck her in I go back downstairs.
I go into the kitchen and rummage through the
knife drawer.
I grab a knife and shut the drawer.
I go back up into my room
and put the knife underneath my pillow.

IN THE WOODS...

JANE'S DREAM

☾

"No—

GET AWAY FROM ME!"

A girl screams and cries for help as she runs through…

The woods.

The forest.

The trees and grasses are grabbing at her as if they want
to pull her

deeper

into

the

woods.

Ta-

tum-

ta-

tum-

ta-

tum.

The Monster is getting closer
and

closer.

She sees a silhouette—

an outline of a tall man coming towards her.

She is about to die.

Ta-
tum-
ta-
tum-
ta-

She screams.

I wake up,
I jump up in a cold sweat.
I am shaking, and my head hurts.
My heart feels like it will leap out of my chest.
My hands are sweating and trembling.
That bad,
bad dream.
Ever since I first heard about the stories,
I've had nightmares.
They are more like night *terrors*.
They seem like they last forever.
Trust me,
they do.
I ask myself:
if something happens to me.
Who would take care of Hazel?

The Date ☾ Jane Nocona

As I get ready to go to the driveway to meet
Harrison I ask myself if this is really a good
idea.
I mean,
yes,
I would say I don't feel threatened around
him.
Nevertheless I am still...

cautious.

He has never done anything bad to me or
another girl...
If he did something bad to another girl I feel
like someone would've told me by now.
Who knows though,
Maybe they don't know if he has done
anything bad and I still don't know what he's
capable of...
    "Jane,
you have fun with Harrison,
mom and I will watch Hazel for you.
She's in good hands."
    "Oh,
I know,

thank you,
Rachel and thank you,
Sarah,"
I say,
 smiling as I put my shoes on.
    "You are welcome,
Jane,
just call or text us if you need anything."
I look up at Sarah again,
smile,
and thank her.
I am about to say something else when a vehicle
pulls up.
It's Harrison.
    "Go,
Jane!
Have a great time!"
she says,
cheerfully and nearly shoves me out of the door.

The Cookout ☾ Harrison John Davis
October 1st, 2022
Custer, South Dakota

We get out of the car and walk towards the
campfire through the thick and smooth smell of
smoke.
     "Hey,
Harrison,
hi,
Jane!"
People yell to us from the campfire.
     We call back to them as we get closer.
          "Is this okay?"
Jane nods her head.
We sit down.
          "Here's a marshmallow,
Jane and a stick for it.
Or do you want a hot dog?"
          "I had dinner already,
I'll just have a marshmallow,"
Jane replied,
handing me a marshmallow.
 Jane texts Rachel and
Sarah to check on Hazel.
Even when Hazel is not with us'
she is always on Jane's mind...

for good reason.

October 7, 2022
Ophiuchus
A Memory

A young girl emerges from the Old Market
passageway.
She walks out of the Old Market..

   "Jane,
are you okay?"
Harrison says,
gently,
but there's a hint of seriousness in his voice.
I nod.
We are walking down passed a poorly lit
alleyway in Rapid City,
the sun is going down fast,
as it is now Autumn.

She wants to go home,
but she's too scared to walk home in the dark.
She's going to catch a ride with a police officer
patrolling the area.
She catches a ride.

I feel myself beginning to tremble.
He looks at me-
puzzled.
   "Are you *sure* you're okay?
You aren't acting right."
   "No,
 no really,
Harrison,

I'm fine."
　"Hold my hand?"
He reaches his hand over to me.
I put my hand into his and we continue to walk.

A few minutes had passed and twelve-
year-
old Jane is sitting
beside a male police officer.
Out of the middle of nowhere,
he grabbed her hair.

I wince and grind my teeth.
　"My god."
I mutter.
He gently grabs my arms.
I lean into him.
　"Jane."
He holds me close to him.
It's night in Rapid City right now.
We are standing across the street from his
pickup.
　"Let's go to my truck,
we need to get you home.
Hazel will be wondering where her mommy is.
She needs you."
I nod and he mutters under his breath and begin
walking me to his truck.
Hazel.

Hazel.

The girl in the police car fights back.

No!

She cries.

*She pushes the officer away from her and tries to open the
door to get out.*

He is far,

far too strong for her.

She can't fight back.

"H-

Harrison,

please,

I need to go home now,

I'm sorry."

"I know,

I'm taking you home."

Click.

He picks me up and puts me into the car.

I start breathing hard.

"Oh god,

I am going to throw up."

I stumble out of the truck.

I fall out of the truck.

I vomit.

The officer grabs the girl's face
roughly.

"Don't even try to get out the car,
you aren't going anywhere,

you silly girl."

I scream and cry.
Tears stream down my face.
I get up onto my hands and knees.
He gently touches my back.
    "G-
get away from me."
I say as if I'm gasping for breath.
I get onto my knees and get up.
Harrison looks shocked.
    "What happened there,
Jane."
I don't say anything.
I continue to stare at him.
Then we hear a motor engine of a vehicle nearby.
It's getting closer.
My heart feels like it just drops out of my chest
and onto the cement in the parking lot.
It's a police car.
I freeze and look up at the
Black Hills night sky.
My heart stops at the sight of a constellation...
Ophiuchus.

The last time when I saw *Ophinchus* was when I was younger,
tonight I feel sick seeing it again,
I promised myself I would never see it.
But I cannot forget that night,
that memory
never.
Never.

After School ☽ *Jane Nocona*
October 5, 2022

I am in eight period,
World History.
Harrison comes over and sits down next to
me.
  "Jane,
I really think that we should talk about
what happened?"
I just look at him,
unsure of what to say.
I just nod my head.
  "B-
but what about Hazel?"
  "She's at the daycare?"
  "Yeah."
  "How about you take her home
first and then we go to meet at the
skateboarding park nearby."

After I drop Hazel off at the Henderson's I go
to the skateboarding park nearby,
behind Hennie's Ice Cream.
I sit down on a ramp looking into the
wilderness.
 The sun is beginning to set behind the trees and
mountains.

I pull my jean jacket more over my thin shoulders
and pull out my phone to message Harrison.
I look over my shoulder behind me and see
him.
I get up,
walk over to him,
and hug him.
    "Let's sit down and talk.
I promise I won't keep you away from Hazel for too
long."
    "Okay."
We sit down facing the sunset.
    "So,
I was just wondering if I did something that
upset you during our date on Friday night."
    "No,
Harrison,
it wasn't you.
It was just a memory that I had."
We sit in silence for a while.
All is silent except for a raven calling in the

distance and crickets and frogs making noise.

    "I don't want to talk about it now,
but I will tell you later."
He wraps his arms around me.

    "I just started remembering more and more
about it."
He doesn't say anything,
he seems like he's listening.

9

The Argument and Declaration ☾ *Jane Nocona*
November 4, 2022
Custer Cougars Football Field

"Good job,
Harrison."
"Thanks."
Thank you for coming."
He smiles and wraps his arm around me.
I wrap my arms around him.
His neck and hair are all wet from sweat.
"You are welcome."
"I love you,
Jane. "
I stare up at him.
He stares back down at me.
"Well...
I'm going to go change.

You just wait here.
You can just wait in my pick up."
He hands me his keys.
  "I love you too."
I say,
watching him walk back behind the school
and beside the practice field to the boys locker
room.
I take them out and get into the car.
I call Sarah on the phone.
Ring.
Ring.
Clink.
  "Hey,
Jane.
How was the game?"
  "It was really good,
how's Hazel?"
"She's good,
she's asleep now."
"Oh,
good.
Thank you for watching her."
  "Wasn't a problem,
Jane.
Just thought you should spend time with your
friends and have fun at the game."
  "I know.
I am going to be home soon.

Maybe a little after nine-
thirty."
   "Alrighty,
thanks."
We hang up.
I jerk my head around.
   "What the-!"
There's a commotion happening outside of the car.
I look around.
I can't see very well even with lights around the parking
lot.
A light flickers out.
I get out of the car.
I hear Harrison yelling.
   "SHUT UP!
HOW DARE YOU USE THAT AWFUL WORD
ABOUT MY GIRLFRIEND!"
I jerk my head around.
   "Harrison?"
I mutter to myself.
I hear a thud.
I rush over to the side of the school.
   "If you ever call Jane that again,
I will-."
The boy standing next to Harrison says it again.
I hear it loud and clearly.
I ball my fists.
My nails go so deep into my skin that I feel blood
trickling onto my fingernails.

"SHUT UP!"

I bark not realizing how loud I truly am.

The boy says something else that I am not able to
make out.

"C'mon,

Jane."

Harrison says,

through gritted teeth,

grabbing my hand.

He let's go of my hand and wraps his arm

around my waist.

His grip is frim but gentle.

The boy follows us.

He whispers,

"Don't listen to him,

Jane,

he doesn't know what the hell he's saying."

"What are you saying to her?

Sweet nothings."

"Get in the car,

Jane."

I get in the car.

Harrison stands in front of the side I am in as if he's
protecting me.

"You dating her is a disgrace to the football
team!"

"No one can tell me who I can and can't date,
including you!

Why would dating her be a disgrace to the

football team,
Buster?"
  "Because she's a freaking mom!
How old is she?
Seventeen?
Sixteen?
She's same age as you,
Harrison!"
The boy leaves and Harrison opens the car door.
  "You can get out now Jane,
you're safe."
I get out.
Harrison covers his mouth and looks like he's sweaty.
  "Come here,
Janet."
He says,
extending his arms to me.

2023

☾

We Aren't Here to Punish You,
We Are Here to Help You ☾ Jane Nocona
March 23, 2023
Custer, South Dakota

"Jane,
we need to talk."
I look up at Mr. Henderson.
   "You are not in trouble,
I just want to talk to you about something."
I follow him into another room.
He holds his office door open for me.
   "Thank you."
I say,
quietly.
 He shuts the door.
My heart skips a beat.
   "Sit down."
I sit down and he sits down in a chair facing me
from across the mahogany table.
   "I found this."
He pulls out a pill.
My heart feels like it has fallen out of my chest and
into my stomach.
I avoid looking back at him,
but I know that he's looking at me.
He's not staring at me like how everyone else does.

It's just different.
I feel different now.
I don't know why I feel that way,
maybe it's because Mr. Henderson wants to help
me.
Am I being seen,
finally?
After all of this time?
Is this how it feels to be seen?
After a long silence,
I look at him strangely because he's a cop.
Aren't the cops supposed to arrest and punish those
who break the rules?
Am I wrong?
Instead of yelling at me and slapping the handcuffs
on me he calmly says,
    "Jane,
is this yours?
Be honest with me,
so that I can help you.
Don't lie."
I nod my head.
    "I'm so sorry."
I burst into tears.
I did it.
I relapsed.
Relapsing is one of my greatest fears.
    "Are there more?"
    "In my backpack.

"Please bring it,
Jane."
I leave the room.
Trembling.
Shaking.
I open it up and dump it on the table.
"Jane."
"I'm so sorry,
Mr. Henderson,
I swear that I tried to stop,
but I relapsed."
"Jane,
my family and I are going to help you,
okay?"
I roll my eyes.
   "Jane,
don't be like that.
I really want to help you because when I look at you
I see a future.
I see a person,
a good person who has the determination to have a
good life.
Do you want a good life?
   "Are you going to put the handcuffs on me
or what?"
   "Jane,
please,
I am not going to punish you,
okay?

I want to help you.
My family and I will help you because,
you have suffered long enough."
You are a smart person.
I saw that you were on the honor all throughout middle
school until the eighth grade.
Do you want your daughter Hazel to have a good
life?
She looks up to you,
you know?
You are her mother.
You are a god to her."
    "Yes,
I guess.
Yes,
I do."
    "Jane,
look at me when I say this,
I know that you love Hazel very,
very much,
okay?
I know that.
You also have to care for yourself in order to care
for Hazel.
If you want to live to see Hazel turn one and you
want to live to see yourself turn nineteen,
you have to stop.
Now.
If you overdose,

Jane,
you will die."
I look down.
If I die of an overdose,
who would take care of Hazel?
    "I don't want to and I am not going to punish
you,
Jane,
okay,
look,
as I said before,
I hate to see people,
especially,
young people like you suffer and you have suffered
long enough."
    "Thank you."
    "You are welcome."

I Want to know How
Did This Happen? ☾ Jane Nocona

asked Mr. Henderson.

"What caused you to start?"

"Yes."

I say,

trying not to cry.

"Do you want to talk about it?"

"It'll m-

make you m-

mad."

He leaned closer to me from across the

dining table.

"Why would it make me mad?"

He asks slowly and in a deep tone.

"I-

I,

because y-

you're a police officer."

"Did a cop do *something* to you?

Is that why you were so terrified when you

saw me the first day you were here?"

He asked.

That's when all of my emotions and anguish

came gushing out of me.

"I-

I'm sorry,
Mr. Henderson."
My lips trembled.
     "That's why I started and why I've been
so afraid of police officers and why I was so afraid
of you when I first saw you."
I lower my head and put it into my hands.
I grip my hair.
     "I'm sorry,
it's just that you are the first police officer who has
ever truly cared about me and who wants to help
me.
 It means a lot."
He nods his head.
     "I'm sorry if it seems like I hate all police
officers!
I don't!
Or well,
maybe a few,
but I don't hate you."
     "I know,
Jane,
I know you don't hate me,
I'm really sorry that you have gone through all of this."
I wipe tears away from my eyes.
I wish that I can say more to him,
but all I can do is just nod my head and think about
what I should have done.
I know that I should've talked to Lydia about it.

I felt I couldn't for some reason.

I did not tell Clara who-
who was like my protector because she "aged out" of
the foster care system.

Then,
all I had was Hazel's father and his crowd.

Ice Cream ☾ Jane Nocona
May 13, 2023
Hennie's Ice Cream Shop
Custer, South Dakota

Rachel and I
(with Hazel in my pack)
walk to Hennie's Ice Cream Shop
to celebrate graduation.
The ice cream store is a tall
brick building near the skateboarding
park.
    "Here,"
I hold the door open.
    "What do you usually get?"
I ask Rachel.
    "The Strawberry Banana or
Caramel and Cashew.
They're both really good.
Get whatever you want."
    "I can pay this time,
Rachel."
    "*Jaaannnnne.*"
    "It's *only* fair that I do.
You and your family have done so much for
us,"
I say.

"HEY!
You just yeeted my wallet!"
We both laugh.
"Seriously,
Rachel,
I'll pay,
I work at the Black Hills Coffeehouse now
trying to make a life for Hazel and me."
She sighs.
We get our ice cream and sit down.
"Cheers,"
we say as we toast with our ice creams.
"Which one did you end up getting?"
"The Strawberry Banana.
What about you?"
"The Caramel Cashew.
What about Hazel?"
"Mango,
she loves licking the spoon!"

10

Another One Gone ☾ *Jane Nocona*
May 31, 2023
Custer, South Dakota

I am sitting in the family room on their white
fluffy rug.
Hazel is lying on her back.
I tickle her.
She laughs joyfully.
She is just over one year old now.
"HAHAHAHAHA!
I laugh too.
My hair falls on her face.
She gets up and climbs into my lap.
I pull her up against my chest.
She turns to face the TV screen.
We have been watching *Spirit:
Stallion of Cimarron,*
but ads start...

"Your show will come back on soon,
honey."
A news flash begins.
"Lila Wolfe was last seen nine months
ago walking along a highway near the Pine
Ridge Reservation in Manderson-
White Horse Creek,
South Dakota."
I cover Hazel's eyes and move my free hand
around to find the remote.
I quickly shut off the TV.
Not
another one gone...
There's too many,
so many we can't keep track anymore.
Being an Indigenous woman in America is
dangerous,
very dangerous...
I feel as though I am a moving target.
I truly feel it!
Too many Indigenous women,
men,
girls,
and boys are going missing every single day.

I I

If Something Happens ☾ *Jane Nocona*
June 4th, 2023

The foster care system decided it was time for me
to leave.
The Henderson's could no longer be a family for
me...
on paper anyway.
I was given a short time to pack our bags and
prepare to leave.
It was time to say goodbye,
and Sarah was trying to reassure me.
    "Jane,
please,
if there's ever a time that you need help,
we'll help you."
I nod my head.
    "Thank you."

Rachel begins to cry and wraps her arms around
me.
    "We will talk on the phone and Facetime.
I promise!"
I try to smile through tears.
Instead I look like I am cringing.
    "Jane,
I have something for you."
    "I have something for you too."
Rachel pulls out a small black box and hands it
to me.
Her hands are trembling.
I take it.
She wipes tears from her eyes.
    "Aw,
Rachel,"
I say,
pulling out a beautiful rose gold necklace.
    "I-
I know that you have always liked that necklace."
    "I have something for you too,"
I say,
taking off my backpack.
I hand her my gift with a cloth wrapped around
it.
She carefully peels off the layers...
    "Oooo.
Such a pretty rock,
it's my favorite color.

What kind of rock is it?"
asks Rachel.

"It's a Rose Quartz."

"Ooooo.
I've heard of those."

"I know that a rock is a strange gift,
but it has special meaning,"
I say.

"What is it?"

"Friendship and healing.
Thank you for being my friend,
Rachel."

"Thank *you*,
Jane."
We stand there hugging each other.
The social worker who was required to come
doesn't know what to do,
she's expressionless.
Rachel's parents stand there not moving.

"Oh Jane,"
Sarah says.
Raymond puts his hand on his wife's shoulder.
Rachel briefly lets me go to hug her parents.
Her hand is still on my back.

"Thanks for everything,
Sarah."
We hug.

"Thank you for helping me to feel...
normal,"

I say.

She hugs me tightly and rubs my back.

I look up at Raymond and try to smile through tears.

He begins to tear up too.

He gives me a hug.

   "Thanks for everything,
Raymond."

   "Oh Jane,
you are welcome.

Take care of yourself, and take care of Hazel.

I know you love her,

and she loves you too."

   "I will."

I try to smile at all of them.

   "O-

H-

Hazel.

I-

I'll really miss you too,"

Rachel says,

moving closer to Hazel and me.

She gently holds her little hands.

   "H-

hard to believe that you are a year old now."

Rachel and I hug again.

   "I really don't want to say goodbye to you,
Jane!"

I look sadly at her and feel as though I'm about to cry again.

I've already cried hundreds of times before today, if not thousands.

12

"I'm
already
gone."

The letter ☾ Jane Nocona
June 4th, 2023

Before I left their home,
I wrote a letter.
I put it under Rachel's book.
I knew she would find it.
But not right away...

Dear Rachel and Family,

Please, if something goes wrong, please look for me. I am not asking you to find me, just to try. I understand, not all people who are missing are found. Do not blame yourselves for what happened to me while I was staying with you. I had a good life because of you. Thank you for all that you have done for me.

Lot's of love, Jane and Hazel.

13

⚜

Facetime ☾ Rachel Henderson
June 5th, 2023

I text Jane
to confirm we will still Facetime.
Me: Is 9 still going to work for
you?
Jane: Yes.
Me: Okay! I'll call you.
Jane: Okay!
Nine o'clock comes around.
I take my mom's Mac computer into
the kitchen and dial up Jane and Hazel.
Ring.
Ring.
Jane answers.
   "Hey!
Rachel!"
   "Hi,
Jane!"

We smile and wave at each other.
    "How was the drive to Deadwood?"
    "It was good...
beautiful scenery.
Hazel slept most of the way."
    "Oh good.
Well,
we miss you both very,
very much."
    "I know,
I know,"
I say,
nodding my head.
    "Hazel and I miss you and your family too."
We talk for hours until it was time for Rachel
to go to bed.
I tell her about my new job,
but there was so much more I could say.

14

⚬〰⚬

Preposterous ☾ *Rachel Henderson*
October 12, 2023
Custer, South Dakota

"Jane,
seriously,
what is going on?
Something is wrong.
I can tell...
even on Facetime."

"Is it something at your job?
You've been acting very strange ever since
you started working in Rapid City."

"I am scared that y-
you won't look for me if I disappear and
y-
you w-
won't t-
take care of -

of Hazelnut i-
if something happens to me,"
she stammers.
    "Jane,
that's preposterous.
Why would you think that?
Yesterday,
Harrison called me and told me that you
said the same thing.
Trust me.
If you went missing,
we would not leave one stone unturned.
We would look for you!
And we would find you.
    Okay?"
Jane sobs and starts to explain,
    "Kelly is a—."
She stops and starts crying again,
clutching Hazel tightly.
    "Jane,
who is Kelly?
If your life is in danger then I need to know,
so tell me.
Now."
    "I never wanted to say good-
bye to you," she says.
Jane then cuts me off and says something that will
haunt me for the rest of my life...
    "You never ever had to,

Rachel,

                                                    I
                                                    was
                                                    already
                                                    gone..."

She said it once before.
Nevertheless,
it burns the same as the first time.

Jane's Post ☾ Jane Nocona
December 12, 2023

Please don't make up reasons for
why I didn't return.
I would never go willingly.
If I go missing,
please don't make any assumptions.
If I go missing,
please care.
Feel some empathy,
feel what I feel.

15

Christmas ☾ Jane Nocona

On Christmas Eve,
we're heading to Custer.
Harrison is driving Hazel and me.
The snow is falling lightly to the
ground.
    "Do you have the snow tire
guards on?"
He nods his head and runs his
hands through his hair with
snowflakes melting in his hair.
    "Do you need a hat?"
I ask,
bending down,
pulling out his winter hat and handing
it to him.
    "Thank you,
dear,"

he says,
taking it and putting it on.
 "You are welcome."
We drive in silence for a long while.
 "Jane,
you're being quiet.
What are you thinking about?"
 "Just thinking about Hazel,"
I say,
looking straight ahead and then at him
for a brief moment.
He nods.
 "Of course you would,
you're her mother."
 "Don't you?" I ask.
 "Always,
even though I'm not her birth father."
He looks over at me.
 "Does it bother you that you
aren't her birth father?"
 "Oh,
no.
I wished he cared for her.
But I do.
I try to be the best father figure I can for her."
 "I know you do."
 "I just wish that you would tell me about
him."
 "He doesn't matter.

He's no longer in my life or in Hazel's.
It's all you now."
I see him smiling.
I love him.
I love Harrison very much.
The best question he ever asked me was if he
could be a *father figure* to my little Hazelnut.
I've never loved him more.
    "What else are you thinking about?"
I shrug my shoulders.
    "I-"
He takes a deep breath.
Inhale.
Exhale.
Repeat.
    "How far along were you when you learned
you were pregnant?"
    "T-
two months,
around two months.
Maybe it was two months too late."
I feel a tear run down my face,
I brush it away,
I really don't want to cry-
it's Christmas.
    "Oh,
Jane."
He puts his hand on my shoulder and squeezes it.
    "Look at her!

She seems happy now,
she's a happy little girl,
Jane.
I'm sorry that you felt the need to do drugs."
    "I just hope that when she's older she
does better than I did.
I don't want her to fall down
the same hole I did."
I wipe another tear from my eye.
    "You're a good mother,
Jane."
We sit silently for a little.
    "You know,
Jane,
Hazel looks more like you every day."

I Might Not Make
it Back ☾ Jane Nocona
December 28, 2023

I stop at Harrison's house.
I tell him I need to meet someone and
buy groceries.
He agreed to watch Hazel.
I kiss Hazel on the forehead and on
her chubby little cheeks.
I give her a big hug—
the biggest,
the longest,
and the tightest hug.
I kiss Harrison.
He kisses me back.
    "I love you,
Harrison."
He wraps his arms around me and holds
me close.
        "I love you too,
Jane.
I love you very much."
        "I know."
        "Why are you crying?"
        "I'm-
I'm sc-

scared,
Harrison!!"
    "Then don't go!"
    "No,
no,
no,
I have to go.
You don't understand!"
    "What is going on?"
I break from his grip and look for my purse
as I go towards the door.
Harrison calls behind me.
    "Jane,
please,
what is going on?
Please tell me."
    "I-
I-
I need to go,
Harrison."
And with tears in my eyes I walk out the
door.
He follows me out of the house and to the car.
    "Jane,
just tell whoever you need to meet that you
can't go.
Tell them Hazel is sick."
    "I have to go,
Harrison."

I cry as I put the key into the ignition.
I try to shut the door,
but as I am closing it Harrison
catches it.
He exhales loudly.
　　"Where are you going?
You said that you were going to get groceries,
but then you said you were going to meet
someone.
Who is that person?"
　　　"A girl from work."
　　　"What's her name?"
I feel myself going red and white in the face
from embarrassment because I know that I
have to lie in order to keep my baby and my
Harrison safe.
I look down at my feet.
　　"I-
I don't know-
her name,"
I say,
looking up at him sad and frustrated.
　　"Your feet...
You aren't wearing the right shoes for snow.
A big one is coming."
　　"Harrison,
I need to go,
I'm sorry.
I need to go get formula and other stuff for

Hazelnut."
    "Hm..."
he looks sternly and suspiciously at me.
    "I have to go,
she's waiting for me."
I slam
the door
and drive away.

10:00 pm

☽

I am starting to get worried.
She left four hours and thirty minutes
ago.
I am sitting in the rocking chair.
Hazelnut is in my arms and wrapped in
a quilt;
It's draped over my legs.
She wakes up a little and begins to squirm
around like she's a little caterpillar.
   "Are you hungry?
Do you want more milk?"
I take the bottle from the coffee table in the
living room and give it to Hazel.
   "It's ok,
Hazel,"
I say.
But is it?
I wonder...

Something is not right with Jane.
She would've called or texted by now.

16

Never This Late ☾ Rachel Henderson
December 28, 2023

I pick up the phone,
it's Harrison:
    "Rachel,
have you heard from Jane?"
    "No,
why,
what's wrong?"
Harrison replies.
    "She left Hazel here earlier today;
I haven't heard from her and it's ten-
thirty now!
She said she would be back by ten!"
I begin to panic.
    "Oh no,
no,
no,

no,
this can't be happening.
No.
What did she say to you?"
    "She has been afraid...
Today she left Hazel here to run an errand.
She texted from a grocery store in Rapid City."
I feel it...
Immediately.
Something is wrong,
Something is very wrong.
Something terrible has happened to her.
    "I must get help!"

Just Another
Indian Girl ☾ Rachel Henderson
December 29, 2023
Rapid City, South Dakota

My dad and I arrive at the nearest police
station...
    "I would like to report a missing
person."
The officer nods and begins typing...
    "What is her name?"
    "Jane."
    "Last name?"
    "Nocona."
What is her date of birth?"
January 14,
2005."
The officer nods his head.
    "What's her ethnicity?
    "Indigenous,
Native American."
    "Oh,
are you sure she isn't with a friend?
Could she be somewhere having a good time?
Teens often leave for a weekend with friends.
    "She is probably just having fun."
I stare at the officer.

"You have no idea."

"She is my friend!"

My dad identifies himself as a retired police

officer and adds,

"She has a daughter.

She wouldn't stay away willingly,

sir."

Exasperated,

I add that

"I think something awful has happened to

her.

She wouldn't just get up and leave her baby.

Even with a trusted friend."

The officer sighs and rolls his eyes.

"She's probably just running late.

Just give her twenty-

four hours.

If she is not back tomorrow,

come back and we will help you."

My dad and I leave.

I want to scream to the police:

You have no idea who Jane is.

She is the best person ever.

She's the best friend ever.

She's the best mother ever.

She loves her daughter very,

very much.

She wouldn't leave.

I just say-

"*Fine.*"

I mutter under my breath.

"*I'll find her myself.*"

The Days Without
Jane ☾ Rachel Henderson
January 6, 2024
Custer, South Dakota

Get
longer
and
longer.
It's only been a week,
but it feels like years.
The days feel like they're never
ending.
Oh god!
I miss Jane so much!
She has touched many lives.
I have to write...

17

Dear Jane,

We love you.

We know that you wouldn't ever run away, especially because of Hazel. My mom and Harrison are taking good care of her, but she needs you. We will search for you. We will search for you until you are found even if you are a million stars away. We love you very much Jane. You are loved beyond belief. We are fighting just as hard as you are. Never stop fighting. No matter how long it takes, we will find you. We will never give up on you.

You don't give up on someone you love.

Rachel

Television Show: The Puzzle of Justice
What caused Jane to Become a Target
and a Tragic and Grim Statistic?
March 1, 2024

The host: "Today on 'The Puzzle of Justice,'
we will be discussing the mysterious and tragic
disappearance of a young mother named
Jane Nocona.
We will cover the following
topics:
Jane,
herself.
Who wanted to harm her?
What caused her to become a target and why?
What were the events leading up to her
mysterious and tragic disappearance?

What are the theories?
Who are the suspects?
The
9-
1-
1

Call."

The screen flickers.

"On December 28th,
2023,
a young woman named Jane Nocona
vanished in parking lot of a grocery store
in Deadwood,
South Dakota."
*The TV screen shows an aerial video of the eerie
parking lot where she was last seen.*
Then,
a school picture of Jane.

TV Host: "Before we talk about Jane 's tragic
and sudden disappearance,
we must first talk about the most important
thing,
the young woman herself.
Who is she?
Jane Nocona was born on January 14,
2005.
She spent her entire childhood in the foster
care system.
When she was seventeen,
she went to live with the Henderson family
where things finally started to get better for
her.
But most importantly,
she was a mother.

Her daughter was in the day care program at the
high school.
More than anything she wanted to have an
education and a good life for her daughter,
Hazel.
Ms. Nocona was kind and an
attentive student.
Her best subjects in school were English and
chemistry.
Her teachers described her as hardworking.
They said she motivated her classmates and
had a lot going for her.
Instead,
of her wishes being granted,
she became the face of a grim statistic,
a statistic of missing and murdered Indigenous
women and girls.
If,
at any time during this episode,
you have information regarding Jane's case,
call Detective Jonathan Oldenburg at
605-753-8799.
So now we get to the most gut-
wrenching question that the community of Custer,
South Dakota desperately wants to answer,
Who wanted to harm her?
Jane's family and close friends have said that
there were people who scared her.
Jane avoided them when she saw them...

These were older boys that
hung out around the school and who went to the
University of South Dakota.
There was one in particular...
One night Jane sent a text saying that there was a
boy who frightened her at a volleyball tournament.
She asked Raymond Henderson,
to come to get her.
We,
however,
don't know this boy's name.
As of now,
anyone could be responsible for her disappearance.
Anyone in the community could be a suspect.
Now,
we get to the question of why is Jane missing?
Well,
Jane was an at-
risk teen,
which made her more vulnerable to violence.
Could someone in the community have had an
obsession towards Jane and towards Indigenous
women and girls?
Or was Jane's kidnapper a complete stranger?
Her good friend kept in touch with her until she
sent her a disturbing message on Snapchat
with her last known location saying
that she was in fear of her life.
Now we will get into the theories.

The first theory is that she was kidnapped,
held hostage,
murdered,
and her body has been discarded somewhere.
Another theory is that a gang took her and is
trafficking her.
The last theory is she was communicating with
someone
online who lured her and is trafficking her.
As of today,
these are merely theories and speculations.
If you have any information about Jane's
disappearance,
please come forward.
Those who know and love Jane deserve to know
what happened to Jane Nocona."

If She Were Just Dead ☾ *Those Who Love Jane*
Rapid City SD
March 15, 2024

We are sitting in Detective Oldenburg's office in
Rapid City.
Everyone who knows and loves Jane is crying.
 "I wished that we could discuss something other
than this,
but there's something that could
still bring you all some sense of closure."
Detective Oldenburg takes a deep breath.
Inhale.
Exhale.
 "As of today,
the most probable theory regarding Jane's
disappearance is that she was *taken*
into human trafficking."
Raymond wipes tears from his eyes.
Sarah covers her mouth and gasps.
Rachel closes her eyes and covers her mouth as
if she's praying.
 "I know that you all are very upset about
this,
and I know how sensitive this is.

I'm not trying to sugarcoat it,
but it would mean that she's still alive."
　　"I-
I know,"
Raymond says,
with a shaky voice.
　　"If she is being trafficked,
where could she be now?"
　　"Anywhere."
People sniffle and cry a little.
　　"If she's being trafficked would it just be
better if she were dead?
I hate picturing what she could be going
through,"
Kelly cries.
　　"Well..."
Detective Oldenburg goes quiet as if he doesn't
know what to say.
　　"We can't say that for sure right now."
Harrison wipes tears from his eyes and leaves
the room.
　　"Harrison."
No response.
　　"Harrison,
where are you going?"
　　"Just leave me alone."

Your Mind Wanders ☾ *Sarah Henderson*

2028

5 years after Jane's Disappearance

Whenever I start thinking about all the scenarios
that could have happened to Jane,
I begin to feel sick to my stomach.
She could be murdered,
and we just haven't found her body or her killer.
She could be being held against her will, and we
haven't found her.
She could be a victim of trafficking,
and we haven't found her.
Or no one can identify her.
Your mind truly does wander when you think
about what could have happened to your loved
one.
I try to be positive.
It's hard.
It has been five years since she vanished out of
thin air,
and it still hurts.

Estranged ☾ Amethyst
2029

I am sitting in the corner beside a bed.
It is a dirty and smelly motel in an
unknown place.
There are other girls here.
I am naked.
I am starving.
I am thirsty.
I am weak.
I am scared.
Please,
don't
look
away.
I miss my family.
I miss myself.

I am terrible sight yet I am still invisible as air
somehow.
Somebody please see me!
I want to go home!

18

I just want to hold my daughter again and be held by Harrison.

19

2025

NO ANSWERS,

JUST THEORIES.

☾

20

THE PRESS CONFERENCE

NOBODY GOES MISSING THE WAY JANE DID

2025

☾

"The family and friends of Jane Nocona
wanted me to show you all the pictures of her,"
Detective Oldenburg says,
holding the picture in front of him.

"She has been missing for a year and three
months now.
Let's bring Jane home."
The circumstances surrounding Jane's disappearance
are very blurry. What we know for sure is that she called 9-
1-
1
in the moments before she went missing.
The last thing we know for sure is that she was in
Deadwood,
South Dakota,
where she was with an unknown
person."

"As of today,
are there any suspects?"
A reporter asks.

"Yes,
we are looking at a few.
There are three who are the most promising.
Since this is an active case I cannot disclose
any names."

Bells on the Door ☾ *Hazel Rose Nocona*
April 14, 2029

I miss mommy.
I want her to come home.
I want her back.
I took a cow bell
off of a cow at Harry Berry's ranch and put it on
the door.
When it rings I can hear and can welcome
her home.
It rings, and I do answer,
but it's never mommy.
When it happens,
I wonder where she is.
I miss her very,
very much.
I want my mommy back.

21

Every Single Lead ☽ *Rachel Henderson*
May 1, 2025
Cody, Wyoming

"What do we do now!?
We have followed every single lead.
They have been dead ends."
Silence.
        "We can't just give up on Jane!
We are the only people she has!
She is the best friend I have!
And what about Hazel?
I really don't want Jane's case to go cold like almost
all of the other cases."
        "Rachel,"
Detective Oldenburg says,
        "I really hate breaking this to you,
but her case has already gone cold.
Her case was cold early on.

There's not a lot we can do except follow through again on what we have already done."

"It's worth a shot.

Let's give it a shot.

Jane is worth it.

A case only goes cold if you stop investigating."

The Promise I Made
to Jane ☾ Rachel Henderson

is a promise I cannot break.
She begged me,
literally,
begged me
to go looking for her
if something happened to her.
At first,
I thought she was paranoid.
Her pleading was something much more
sinister.
She had a very real fear of being stolen.
I can't imagine going around town with a
target on my back.
How scared she must have been when she
was *stolen* for real.
As she always said,
promises are promises and promises are
unbreakable.

22

Fighting as Hard as We Are ☾ *Rachel Henderson*
2026

When I am getting out of the car I hear
something breaking underneath my
foot.
It sounded like glass.
Since Jane went missing my heart is
sort of like glass.
It could break at any moment.
I look down and cringe.
　　"Ew."
I grimace.
I see a pair of blue
latex surgical gloves.
Tonopah is small,
and I can't help
but feel a sense of uneasiness here.

It feels as if something terrible,
awful,
and sinister has happened here.
As I bend over to pick up the shattered
translucent beer bottle, my strawberry
blonde hair whirls around me like a tornado.
I also feel little hairs rising on the back of my
neck.
We are in Tonopah because there was a tip.
Somebody thought they saw Jane being
dragged into an old mine shaft.
She was dead.
I hope they were wrong.
I hope she was just *playing* dead.
We walk into the mine shaft.
It's dark and chilly inside.
I turn on my headlamp and continue to follow
my family,
Harrison,
and some volunteer search members.
    "So,
where did they see her being dragged?"
        "From that the hill there by that
car,"
Harrison says,
pointing to a sand dune like area.
        "It would be close to that cul-
de-
sac."

After Harrison finishes talking he begins to look as if he's about

to cry, his mouth is trembling like he's about to cry,

but it's also out of anger and probably love for Jane and Hazel too.

Of course,

Hazel.

Little Hazelnut.

23

In the data...
We just fall through the cracks.
Down.
Down.
Down.
We go falling.
Like we're falling in a free fall.
Some don't care enough
to plug our cases into the
National Missing and Murdered Persons
Database.
I wished they would care.

Looking For Jane—
Alive ☾ Detective Oldenburg

I want to find Jane.
I want to find Jane
alive.
I hope to find Jane
alive
even though the chances of finding her alive
are getting
                    smaller
and
                    smaller every single day
she's
missing.
I have to search for Jane and keep
the hope alive for those who love her very,
very
much.

24

PART TWO

PINK MOON RISING

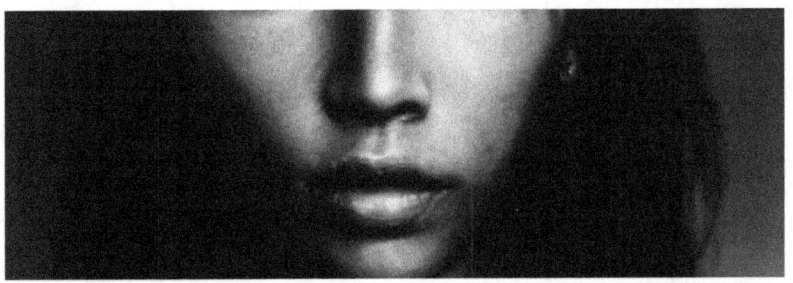

Her Biological Family ☾ Rachel Henderson
March 21, 2025

We are at a cafe in Niobrara,
Nebraska having dinner with Jane's older
cousin,
     Alyssa...
When Jane went missing,
Lydia,
from the the foster care agency,
was able to put us in touch with Jane's cousin.
    "Is she here?"
My dad asks,
looking over at my mom.
She checks her phone and nods.
As mom looks up from her phone,
a tall woman waves to us.
She looks like Jane...
We walk to her and sit down.
    "Thank you for taking care of Nokomis."
Nokomis?
    "Her real name was Nokomis?"
The woman nods.
    "*Jane* was a name the foster
care center gave her."
    "Oh,"
I say,

looking down at the menu.
We sit there just staring at each other for a while.
    "Thank you.
Thank you so much for what you did for her,"
Alyssa said.
    "Thank you for taking her in,
for caring for her,
and for loving her as much as you all did.
And thank you for reporting her missing.
I doubt that she would have been reported if she
weren't with you."
We show each other pictures and both learn
about her,
oh,
so much about her.
I almost feel like I didn't know her at all when
she lived with my family and me.
There's a lot that I truly didn't know about her.
Her childhood was tougher than I thought.
There were a lot questions that Alyssa
asked that I could not answer.
I wished I knew the answers to those questions.
I also had questions for Alyssa... many she could
not answer.
I showed Alyssa a picture of Nokomis holding Hazel
for the first time.
That picture holds a special place in my heart.
    "Aw,"
she smiles and flips it over.

"She's beautiful.

Wow!

She looks just like Jane when she was a baby.

You know,

Rachel,

Jane looks so much like her mother,

Star."

Star is Nokomis' biological mother.

"Did Nokomis have any brothers or sisters?"

"No,

but she had you,

Rachel.

She was one of the few lucky ones.

When you were hosting Jane and Hazel,

what was she like?"

"She was lovely,"

my mother chimes in.

"She was a lovely girl."

"She was like a big sister to me,

really she was,"

I say.

Alyssa smiles.

25

TWELVE WEEKS LATER...

☾

Television Show: "The Puzzle of Justice"
Jane's Past: The Truths in Between
March 1, 2025

"On tonight's episode of 'The Puzzle of Justice,"
we will re-
examine the tragic and mysterious disappearance
of Jane Nocona.
If you have been following her case,
you would have heard that her name is *not*
Jane Nocona,
it is Nokomis Nagua.
Her time in foster care is still shrouded in mystery
like the woman herself.
But the answers her families so desperately want
may be presented tonight!
We have a special guest who knew Nokomis in
foster care."
The screen flickers.
On view is a room with two chairs and two small
coffee tables side-
by-
side.

"What was Jane like when you knew her?"
"She was the sweetest thing ever...
clever and
sensitive.

She thought about others.
She took care of me,
and I took care of her.
I remember when her best friend Clara J. Morrison
left.
Honestly,
Jane was terrified.
A gang took her in.
She didn't want to join,
but I think she felt like she wanted and needed to be
protected,
you know?"

"She felt endangered then?"

"One-
hundred percent!

"Were there any people who she was afraid
of?"

"Yes.
There were."

"Do you know who?"
The girl has a sad look on her face and begins to
fidget uneasily.

"Yes,
the police.
She was terrified of them."

"Did she ever trust them?"

"She did before a male police officer did
something just awful to her.
She was raped.

She only told me.
I really,
truly believe that's why she fell off the right path."
Silence.
    "She had a lot of anger in her.
She was hurting.
Not just because of her own personal trauma,
it was also shared trauma.
She didn't know how to handle it and what
happened next was very,
very sad.
I wished that I could have helped her more.
She knew that she had a problem.
She really wanted
to get out of that black hole she was in.
It's so sad,
she was–
you know,
it got to a point where she couldn't stop it.
Trust me,
it tore her apart.
She wanted a good life, and she was trying to get
out of it about when she left to go
live with the Hendersons."
    "How old was she when this started?"
    "Twelve turning thirteen."
    "Where did she get the money for the
drugs?"
    "I-

I really don't know.
I didn't know that she was addicted until the time
when she asked for help."
The interviewer nods her head.
    "And what about Hazel?
Do you know who Hazel's biological father is?"
The girl closes her eyes.
    "He doesn't matter,"
the girl says,
nodding.
    "Nokomis said that to you?"
    "Yes,
she did."
    "What are your opinions about the
theories?"
        "I believe she was *lured* into
trafficking somehow.
Or,
perhaps she was *abducted* into that twisted,
dark underworld...
maybe *both*."
The interviewer nods her head.
        "I have a lot of questions about what
happened that night."
        "Do you think you may know who
did this?"
The girl shrugs her shoulders,
        "Just like everyone else,
ma'am,

I wish I knew."

She Did It ☾ *Rachel Henderson*

It hits me like a brick...
Kelly...
she has something to do with this!
I leave the TV on and
grab my phone.
Me: Kelly!
Kelly: Heyyyyyyyyy.
Me: I don't have time for this,
Kelly.
We need to talk;
what did you do to my friend?
Kelly: Say that again?
Me: What.
Did.
You.
Do.
To.
My.
Friend?
Kelly: Rachel,
if you meet me at the Blue Bell Lodge
campgrounds,
I will tell you what I can.

I Know What You Did ☾ *Rachel Henderson*

January 1, 2026

Somewhere
in South Dakota in the Woods

"I know you did something to Jane,"
I say,
following her.
She looks at me with a smirk on her face that breaks
into laughter.
"You and Guy did something."
At least one other person was with her that night."
"What makes you think I did something to her?"
"Harrison texted me and asked if I remember Jane,
or I mean Nokomis now saying she was going out
with a female friend.
And who was the other 'female friend' besides me who
she trusted?
Hm!"
I say,
beginning to lose my temper and pointing at her.
"What did she do that was so terrible?
That you had to trick her?
All she was doing was getting groceries for Hazel."
My voice breaks when I think about Hazel.

Hazel.

"No two-
year-
old should ever live without a mother.
You deceived her didn't you?
God forbid what's happening to her now!"
I look deep into her eyes.
The same set of eyes that Nokomis saw when she
vanished out of thin air.

"Everyone knows that she's being trafficked,
everyone in this whole town,
Kelly."
Kelly looks like she's trying to act innocent.
She is not,
she is guiltier than sin; I know it.

"She trusted you and then you betrayed her."
I start walking away from her,
behind my shoulder I call,

"Kelly!

IF YOU TRULY CARE ABOUT HER YOU TELL ME
WHERE
THE HELL SHE IS AND WHAT IS HAPPENING TO
HER!
DO YOU HEAR ME!?"
I begin sobbing.

"Y-
Y-
YOU ARE A HORRIBLE PERSON!"
She comes charging at me.

She hits me across the face and knocks me to the ground.
I feel blood trickling out of my mouth.
I can taste it.
I look up at her angrily.

"Was this what you did to her!
Huh?
Did you hit her and knock her to the ground?
Did you make her bleed and cry!?"
She pulls my hair.
I punch her face as hard as I can.
I feel the bones in her nose breaking and wetness on her face.
She runs away.

26

Pretend She's Someone Else
Colder Than Cold - Jane Nocona

☾

27

The Interview ☾ Rachel Henderson &
Raymond Henderson

Birds sing.
Rachel brushes her hand along the prairie grass and
wildflowers.
"It's been very hard on us ever since she went
missing.
It's been especially hard on my dad.
Um,
w-
we miss her.
We want her back.
We want her to come home."
The screen switches to Raymond with a black
backdrop behind him.
"Every day we search for her,
and find almost nothing.
Whenever we go out searching,

*I always trick myself into thinking that I am just
searching for another young lady-
a stranger.
It's another ballgame
having a missing family member.
It's a lot different than seeing a picture of a stranger
on the news.
It's been very hard."*

28

WE MAY NEVER SEE HER AGAIN

COLDER THAN COLD - JANE NOCONA

2028

☾

29

"The hardest part is that y-
you might never see them again,
especially if the case has gone *cold*."
    "I-
this is going sound bizarre to some,
but it's the truth.
I-
um see her *everywhere*,
I see her on the tv,
I see her in the paper,
I see her in...
oh God,
all sorts of things.
This happens all the time when I am
walking alone.
I trick myself into thinking I've seen her.
But it's never her,
it's always a dream."

30

She's Probably Dead
Colder Than Cold - Jane Nocona

2029

☾

31

On the TV screen,
Harrison is standing in a wheat field at his ranch in
Deadwood,
South Dakota.
He is holding hands with Hazel who is now seven.
A flower blows across the screen...

"A part me believes that Jane is still alive,
that's she is still here...
But, because of all the rumors,
it seems almost impossible that she's still h-
here.
Of course I want her to be alive,
but if she's in pain-
I-
I just don't want her to suffer anymore.
She is missed and loved very much."
The TV screen flickers to an aerial shot of
Custer,
South Dakota and then in front of the

Henderson Family Home.

"A part me believes that she will just
randomly appear in Custer or maybe in the
coffeehouse where we
hung out or just randomly,
you know,
walking around.
Another part of me thinks that she is dead
somewhere...
maybe in the woods or in the mountains or in
an abandoned building.
As of now,
I hate to say it,
she's

                       probably

dead."

An Arrest ☾ The Puzzle of Justice

The TV Host comes into view.

"It's been over five years since Jane Nocona
went missing...

There has been a recent arrest for sex trafficking.
Just last week,
Guy Stewart was arrested on charges of
sex trafficking and running a ring
throughout the states.
He is in questioning...
If at any time you have information that could be
related to the Nacona case,
please
come forward."

32

SHE WAS *CONVENIENT*

THE INTERROGATION ROOM

(PART ONE)

2029

☾

33

"Why Jane?
Why would you target her?"
He leans back and crosses his large,
tattooed arms around his chest.
He sits there a minute and then throws his head
back and laughs.
   "She was convenient.
That's why."
      "Convenient?"
      "Yes,
She was very convenient.
She was perfect.
Why wouldn't I have targeted her?"
Silence.
      "We made a lot of money off her."
      "It wasn't my fault,
it was her fault.
I-
you know.

She reminds me of a baby zebra walking in front of
a lion."

The private detective stares at him.

"So,
you're telling me that when a baby zebra walks
in front of a lion,
is it the zebra's fault if they are eaten?"

"Yes."

"She didn't know what you and Kelly were
going to do to her at the parking lot,
right?
Tell me what happened to her in the parking lot?"

He laughs again.

"She didn't go willingly."

"Didn't she?
Did you threaten her?"

We stare at each other for what seems to be hours.

"I did.
I threatened her multiple times and scared her so
she would not tell the people she trusted."

"How did you lure her?"

"Through Kelly and the internet."

Detective Oldenburg looks up from his notes.

His eyes are narrowed.

"Kelly?
Kelly who?"

A big smirk appears on his face.

Hazel's Drawing ☾ Harrison John Davis
2029

"Can I show you what I drew at
school,"
Hazel asks.
"*Sure,*"
I grin.
She digs through her small pink backpack and pulls out a
piece of paper.
Hazel drew three stick figures:
one of herself,
one of *daddy*
(me),
and one of mommy.
Daddy. Me. Mommy.
"Your mom would love this,
Hazelnut."
She nods.
"Did mommy love me?
I hoped she loved me because I love her,
and I miss her."
I bend over and look her in her eyes,
"Hazel,
of course
she loves you!
You are her daughter!'

"But s-
she isn't here.
She didn't come to my birthday."
She says,
tearfully.
    "Will she come back home?"
    "Oh,
she will,
Hazel,
she will."
She has to come home.
I tell myself.

34

You Gotta Be Tough ☾ Rachel Henderson

"Tell me more about Jane,
I mean Nokomis,
when she was born,"
I ask Alyssa.
　"I didn't see her when she was born;
I only saw one picture.
It was of her mother.
Star left her at a fire station in Omaha,
Nebraska."
　"Oh,"
I say,
looking at the picture of her standing next to
Hazel in the pot when we were making cookies
together.
　"I'm sorry."
　"Me too,"
Alyssa says,

nodding her head.

    "Her childhood was a lot tougher than I thought it was."

    "Yes.

It was.

Ever since Star told me that she surrendered her baby,

I've always wanted to know what happened to her."

We smile,

shyly,

at each other.

    "Tell me about Nokomis when she lived with you and your family,"

Alyssa asks.

    "Oh,

wow,

well,

she is impossible

to forget...

so was Hazel.

I love her,

and she was my best friend.

She was also tough.

She was the toughest person I've ever met."

    "I know,

Rachel,

for better or for worse,

you've gotta be tough

in this world."

35

***

Hazel's Dream ☾ Harrison John Davis
February 14th, 2029
Hazel and I are in the kitchen

today is Valentine's Day.
I look at her as she gobbles down her breakfast.
　"Honey,
your hair is getting into your food."
　　"Oops."
She flips her hair over her tiny shoulder the
same way Jane did.
We are eating oatmeal with raisins.
We eat quietly for a little while.
　　"Hazel,
honey."
　　　"Yes,
daddy?"
She looks up from her oatmeal with some almond
milk dripping from her chin.

"I'm sorry that your mother isn't here
for Valentine's Day again."
"It's okay,
daddy."
I look at her sadly.
She starts eating her breakfast again.
"You deserve your mother,
and she deserves you."
"Yeah,
I miss mommy.
I hope mommy misses me too."
"She does,
Hazel,
she misses you very much."
After we finish eating,
we do the dishes together.
Hazel looks at me from across the sink after
setting her clean bowl on the counter.
"Hey,
daddy?"
I turn to look at her.
"Yes?"
"I had a dream last night.
Can I tell you about it?
"Sure,
of course.
What happened?"
"Mommy came to visit me in a dream
last night.

Do you want to know what she said?"
    "She asked me to make a wish.
You know what I wished for daddy?"
        "What's that my little Hazelnut?"
        "I told her that I want her to come
home.
And you know what mommy said?"
Hazel
climbs down from the step stool and over to
the chair I am sitting on to get onto my lap.
I pull her up onto my lap.
        "What is that honey?"
        "She said don't worry because I will come
home."
I feel my face turning red and tears
stinging my eyes.
        "What's wrong daddy?
I thought that would make you happy."
        "It did sweetheart,
it did,"
I say as my lips quiver.
        "Mommy loves you so much.
She really does.
I am very sorry she isn't here.
You deserve your mother."
        "She'll be back daddy.
She promised.
A promise is a promise.
Promises are unbreakable."

I hug my little girl and try not to cry in front of her.

36

⚜

Help....
Me...
Please ☾ Anonymous
March 1, 2029
Love's Gas Station
Alliance, Nebraska

I am buying soft drinks and some Reese's
chocolates when I look up.
The sight haunts me.
It will haunt me until my dying day.
A tall slender young woman stands in
front of me.
Her long black hair is matted.
She is only wearing a tank top with a bra strap
falling down one shoulder.
Her denim shorts have sequins on the pockets
and fringe at the hem.

She turns her head to look at me.
I see two black eyes.
She has bruises on her legs,
chest,
arms,
and hands.
She stares at me and mouths something that
looks like.
Help...
me...
please.
Immediately,
I take out my phone to call law enforcement.
When I do,
the girl seems to know what I am doing.
She looks relieved.
She closes her eyes and falls to the floor.

37

On The News ☾ *Tadd Jerkins*
March 2, 2029

News Anchor #1: "Good evening,
a young woman has been found in critical
condition and is suspected to be a victim
of a human trafficking ring."
News Anchor #2: "That's right,
Harriet.
The young woman is thought to be the
eighteen-
year-
old who went missing
on December 28,
2023 named Nokomis Nagua aka Jane Nocona."
My eyes open wide.
She's alive.
I need to call Harrison!
I rush to my phone that's charging in the next

room.

"Harrison,

have you seen the news?"

"No,

I just got up.

Hazel had a bad night."

"They say there's girl in the hospital that

is thought to be...."

"WHAT!!!!!????

What hospital?"

Harrison exclaims.

"I am turning on the news now!

Sorry Tadd,

Detective Oldenburg is calling.

I'll put you on hold."

38

TOGETHER AGAIN

MARCH 3, 2029

ALLIANCE, NEBRASKA

ALLIANCE GENERAL HOSPITAL

☾

39

Her eyes are bruised.
Black.
Dark shades of blue.
Purple.
In some places a musky yellow that looks almost
tan.
She looks a little like a raccoon.
Sarah covers her mouth at the sight of Jane.
Tears roll down her cheeks.
We found her.
We got her.
There are a few people with Jane.
Harrison.
Hazel.
Rachel.
Sarah.
More are coming.
She's in a deep sleep.
Her long beautiful hair is tangled and matted.

Rachel and Harrison stand beside her.
Alyssa stands behind them watching the scene
unfold...
Rachel can't believe her eyes.
She clasps her hands over her mouth.
Harrison bows his head,
wipes away tears and pulls Hazel closer against
his chest with his free arm.
     "C-
can I-
I h-
hold her hand?"
Rachel asks one of Jane's nurses with her bottom
lip trembling.
     "That would be just fine."
Rachel sits down on the edge of the hospital bed
and gently takes her hand.
She begins to cry a little as she holds her hand.
     "It's okay now,
Jane,
you're safe now,"
she says,
rubbing Jane's hand.
     "We-
we got you."
Rachel looks up at the nurse with tears falling
from her eyes.
     "H-
how did she get here?"

"I don't know everything,
but I was told that she was at a gas station in
Alliance,
Nebraska and collapsed."
    "She collapsed!"
Sarah yelps,
covering her mouth in shock.
    "Do you know why she collapsed?"
    "It seems to be extreme exhaustion."
    "Oh God,"
exclaims Harrison.
He gently rests his hand on her forehead
as if he's taking her temperature.
Hazel chimes in,
    "Daddy,
daddy,
is that mommy?"
    "Yes,
honey,
that's mommy."
Her eyes light up and a grin spreads across her
face.
        "SHE CAME HOME!
I-
I KNEW SHE WOULD COME HOME
AGAIN!
Can I hug her daddy!?
Please daddy!
PLEEEEEASE!"

"Yes,
honey,
but be quiet.
She's trying to sleep."
She jumps on the bed next to her.
Jane wakes up with a start.

Awake ☾ Jane
March 3, 2029

I open my eyes...
The bright light against the creamy
white walls is blinding.
I gasp.
    "Hazelnut?"
    "Mommy!

                Mommy!"
Hazel bounces up and down on the bed.
She crashes into my chest and flings her
arms around me.
    "I love you mommy!
Where have you been?
I missed you so much!"
The words are music to my ears.
    "Oh Hazel,
I-
I am so sorry!
You've grown so much.
I hope I didn't hurt you.
I didn't want to leave you....
I'm so so sorry..."
    "Oh,
Jane,
none of this was your fault,"

Harrison says,
moving himself closer to Hazel and me.
He takes me gently
into his arms.
    "We love you,
Jane,
we love you.
We missed you so much,"
he sobs.
Hazel snuggles in between Harrison and me.
    "Don't cry mommy,"
she says,
as she wraps her tiny arms around me.
It was a sad,
but beautiful moment.

Interrogating Suspect #2 ☾ Detective Oldenburg

I am staring at Kelly Johnson in the interrogation
room...
"Do I look like a monster to you?"
she asks.
"I don't know.
What does a monster look like?
Now,
how did you know Jane?"
"From work."
"Where did the two of you work?"
"A coffee shop."
"You knew that she was vulnerable didn't
you?
She trusted you.
But you fooled her.
You lied to her.
You *tricked* her.
You deceived her."
Silence.
She stares at me.
"Was this premeditated?"
I ask.
"No."
"It seems that it was."
"No,

it was not."

"You had your eye on her the whole time didn't you?"

Family Campfire ☾ Harrison John Davis
March 6, 2029
Deadwood, South Dakota

It's been two weeks since Jane has returned
from the hospital.
She's recovering well.
    "Can I tell a story?"
    "Go ahead,
Hazel,"
I say.
    "This is my favorite,
it's about mommy!"
I give Hazel the flashlight to hold near her face.
There once was a little girl named Hazel.
One night,
she was crying
because she missed her mommy.
That night,
She had a dream.
Her mommy
said,
    "Don't cry little one.
I want you to make a wish."
    "I wish my mommy would come home."
You know what my mommy said in my dream?
She made a promise:

"Don't worry;
I'll come home.
A promise is a promise."

I'm Not Afraid of Anything ☾ Jane Deadwood, South Dakota April 1, 2029

Hazel is crying.
She's having a nightmare.
I can hear her from the living room and walk over
to her bedroom to comfort her.
    "I'm afraid,"
she sobs,
grabbing my arm and clinging to me.
    "What happened?"
    "I-
I was having a b-
b-
bad d-
d-
dream."
I hug her and pull her closer.
She wiggles over to me.
I wrap my arms around her.
    "What happened to you in your dream?"
    "I was being taken.
I was being stolen."
I shudder,
and my heart sinks.
I cannot bear the thought of some evil monster

taking my daughter.

"Oh,
Hazel,
I will protect you as long as I am your
mommy."

"And how long is that?"

"Forever!"

She sobs into my chest.

I kiss her lightly on the head.

"I love you,
mommy."

"I love you too,
my little Hazelnut."

We sit there silently for a while.

"Mommy,
are you afraid of anything?"

I think for a moment.

"I am not afraid of anything,
honey."

She looks at me strangely.

"How?"

"I have cheated death.
I am one of the lucky ones."

"How did you cheat death?"

I hold her tightly and squeeze her little hands.

She leans her head on my chest.

"I will save that story for another day
when you're older,
I will tell you.

My life is not what you think it has been before
I came home."
We all have struggles in our lives.
At the end of the day,
we are all stories.
    "I love you,
mommy."
    "I love you too, my sweet little Hazelnut."
I hold her,
and we fall back asleep...

Ready. ☾ Jane
April 10, 2029

I wake up bright and early.
At 6 am.
Sharp.
I take off my night clothes and get into
the shower.
After I turn on the water and wash my
hair I look down at
my body.
My hands.
My arms.
My chest.
I have scars from the trafficking.
Outside.
And inside...
I have a tattoo on my lower back that I want
to remove after the hearing.
I am taking my body back.
My mind?
I don't know.
I get out of the shower and wrap a towel
around me.
I pull it tight.
I sit,
but not for long.

I laid out my black slacks the night before.
I find my red blouse with the ruffles.
I put on my makeup.
But not too much.
Not like before.
It's time.

40

COURTROOM
INTRODUCTION- JANE
APRIL 10, 2029

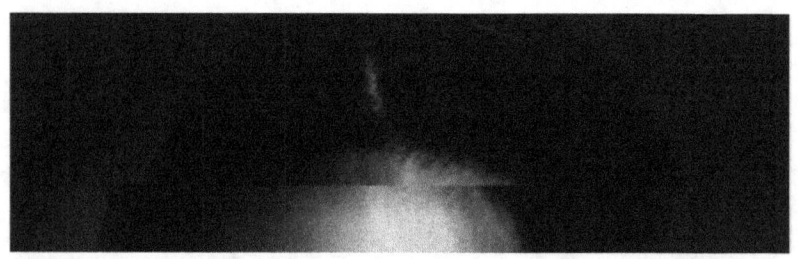

"All rise."

We all stand up.

The judge walks in and sits down in her chair.

"You may be seated,"

she says.

We all sit down.

"Are *they* coming in now?"

I ask my attorney,

Ms. Jones,

in a whisper.

"Soon."

She gives me an encouraging smile.

Suddenly,

I feel very faint and lightheaded.

I feel as though I might throw up.

I bend over and put my hands on the table.

She puts her hand on my back.

"Are you okay?

"Just nervous...

I feel dizzy."

"Are you going to be sick?"

I nod and say,

"Possibly."

A court clerk comes over and asks,

"Shall I get you some water?"

"Please."

He leaves and comes back with a water

bottle.

"Thank you."

"You are welcome."

He walks away.

"Are you going to be okay,
Jane?"

"Yeah,
I will be."

"Ms. Jones,
you may proceed,"
says the judge.

My attorney stands up in front of the court
to give her opening statement.

"My client,
Ms. Nacona
is a hard working young woman who loves
her family,
friends,
community,
and especially her daughter,
Hazel.

Ms. Nacona told me that Hazel
is the most important thing in her life.

Ever since,
she was a young child and as a teen,
she wanted to have a good life.

She was motivated,
but going through multiple families in the foster
care system presented her with challenges.

She was on her way to a life with more stability
and hope,

but on December 28,
2023,
that was taken away from her in a brutal way.
She was lured and kidnapped.
She was trafficked for five years and suffered
immense pain."
        "Thank you,
Ms. Jones,
you may take a seat."
The judge writes something down and looks to
the back of the room.
The opposing attorney,
Mr. Boyce,
steps forward.
        "Mr. Boyce,
you may make your opening statements now."
I am in a daze as *his* attorney speaks.
I have no idea what he says.
I don't *want* to *know* what he is saying.
Finally,
it is our turn.
Ms. Jones,
says,
        "Harrison John Davis,
you may take the stand."
He hands Hazel to Rachel and walks to the
platform to give his statement as a witness.
        "Mr. Davis,
raise your right hand."

He raises his right hand.

"Mr. Davis,
do you solemnly swear that the testimony you are
about to give is the whole truth and nothing,
but the truth,
so help you,
God?"

"I do,"
he says as he nods his head.

"What is your name?"

"Harrison John Davis."

"Mr. Davis,
how did you meet Ms. Nocona?"

"At school;
we went to high school together for our junior and
senior years.
Rachel introduced us."

"When did you two start dating?"

"Junior year,
in the late fall."

"What were you doing the night of
December
28,
2023?"

"Watching Hazel,
Jane's daughter."

"How long did Mrs. Nocona want you to
take care of her?"

"Um,

from seven pm to ten pm."

"What time did Mrs. Nocona say she was coming home?"

"Ten pm."

"You say she was going to come home at ten pm that night just now,
didn't you,
Mr. Davis?"

"Yes."

"At what point in time did you start to get worried that something had happened to her?"

"Oh,
10:05,
because she would call or text when she would be late.
It wasn't like her to be late."

"You tried texting her and calling her,
didn't you?"

"Oh,
yes,
I did."

"And she never answered the calls or texts?

"That is correct."

"What did you do then?"

"I called Rachel and asked if she knew anything."

"What did Rachel tell you?"

"She told me that Jane sent her location on Snapchat."

"Where was the last known place that she was before she went missing?"

"In a parking lot in Deadwood."

"Did you drive out there to look for her?"

"You bet I did.

I was very concerned."

The attorney nods his head and writes something down.

Then looks back up.

"Thank you,

Mr. Davis,

you may take a seat."

"Rachel Evie Henderson,

you may take the stand now."

Rachel walks to the front of the courtroom.

"Ms. Henderson,

raise your right hand."

She raises her right hand.

"Ms. Evie Henderson,

do you solemnly swear that the testimony you are about to give is the whole truth and nothing but the truth,

so help you,

God?"

"I do."

She walks over and sits down.

"What is your name?"

"Rachel Evie Henderson."

"Ms. Henderson,

Mr. Davis stated she texted you just moments before she vanished.

"What did you do after she sent the text with her last known location?"
"I talked to Harrison and called my parents."
"What happened then?"
"We all went to the grocery store."
"What did you and the others find?"
"Her phone with a crushed screen."

41

COURTROOM

BLACKMAIL ☾ JANE

APRIL 11, 2029

Ms. Johnson asks,
    "Ms. Nocona,
can you share the details of what happened in
the parking lot?"
I choke as I begin to talk....
    "Well,
I..."
I brush my hair from my face.
    "Yes,"
I say,
nodding my head.
        "Would you describe those details?"
        "I had just brought groceries and was walking
to my car when I saw that I had a flat tire.
At first I thought that I just ran over a nail or
something.
Then I saw this black pickup truck, and Kelly
roll down the window."
        "What happened after you saw Kelly rolling
down her window?"
        "I walked up to Kelly and asked her to help.
Kelly and I were talking and
then all of the sudden I felt this wall smash into me.
Before I knew it,
I was being dragged into the vehicle."
        "Is it true that you met Ms. Johnson at work?"
        "Yes."
        "Where did you and Ms. Johnson work?"
        "At Starling's Coffee in Rapid City."

"When you first met Ms. Johnson,
is it true that you thought she was nice?
And you trusted her?"
        "Y-
yes."
I nod my head.
        "What was your first thought when she
started blackmailing you?"
        "Betrayed,
Angry.
I wished I had never met her."
        "As you can see here,
Ms. Nocona
did not go willingly. "
Ms. Jones points at the screen showing a text I got
from Kelly:
*If you don't come with me to Rapid City Saturday night,
I will kill Hazel.*
        "As you can see,
she *threatened Ms. Nocona* by telling her that if she
didn't obey her and go to Rapid City that night she
would kill Hazel.
Think for a minute,
jury,
what would you have done if you were in that same
exact situation...
She did go,
but she didn't go willingly.
She went because,

in her own words,
      "I had no choice,
I needed to protect my daughter,
so I went."
The attorney turns off the projector.
      "Recordings Ms. Nocona took also show
the depth of the deception and crime.
Ms. Nagua felt the need to *record* some of her
conversations with Ms. Johnson when she was at
work with her."
Ms. Jones turns on a speaker.
      "I am going to play one of the recordings,
and I am going to tell you now,
they are distrubing."
She looks at the jury grimly.
I feel myself wincing.
I plug my ears.
I don't want to relive those memories.
I keep my head up.
Crackle.
Crackle.
Me: "Kelly,
I am not going to do something I don't want to."
Kelly: "Well,
then...
I will kill Rachel and bury her body where no
one will ever find it.
I know how to make her death look
like an accident.

I know how to cover it up.
No one would ever find her."

COURTROOM

THE 9-1-1 CALL ☾ JANE

APRIL 12, 2029

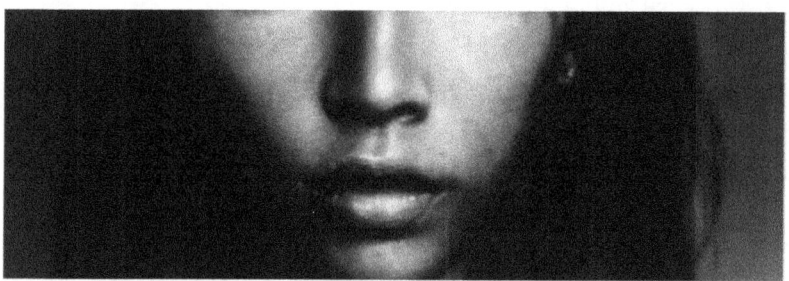

42

"Officer Cunningham has been asked
to testify today.
Officer David Cunningham,
you may take the stand,"
says Ms. Jones.
The Officer takes the stand.
    "David Cunningham,
raise your right hand,"
says the Judge.
He raises his right hand.
    "Mr. Cunningham,
do you solemnly swear that the testimony you
are about to give is the whole truth and
nothing,
but the truth,
so help you,
God?"
    "Yes,"
he says,

nodding.

"Please be seated.
Mr. Cunningham,
on December 28th,
2023 at approximately 10:30 pm,
Ms. Nocona called
9-
1-
1-
You were the dispatcher who answered her call
that night,
is that correct?"

"Yes."

"What did she say?"

"It was hard to make out what she was
saying due to the quality,
but I was able to understand she said help me.
She said help me five times before the line went
dead."

43

COURTROOM
THE IMPACT
STATEMENT ☾ JANE
APRIL 13, 2029

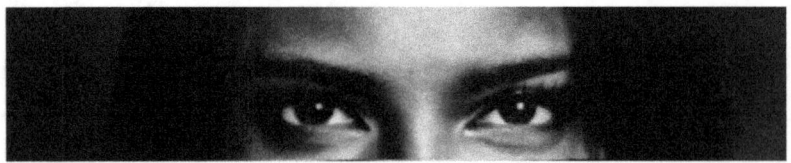

44

We return to the courtroom.
The courthouse is filled with friends and
family...
and advocates of those who have been
trafficked.
I am sitting in the audience with
Harrison,
Alyssa,
Rachel,
and Hazel.
The Judge breaks the silence of the courtroom.
    "Jury,
what is your verdict?"
The juror in the front row,
closest to the judge stands up.
She says,
    "The jury has considered the nature of
this crime to be especially cruel.
We the jury find defendants Guy Stewart

guilty of kidnapping and sex trafficking on
all accounts,
including the murder of Clara J. Morrison
in the second degree.
The jury finds Kelly Johnson guilty of
sex trafficking."

The courthouse erupts.
Jane's family shouts in joy,
and Hazel hugs her mother.

As the crowd starts to become quiet,
the Judge makes her final comments:

The violence against women and girls
everywhere is a significant problem,
but the rates of violence against Indigenous
women and girls is even greater.
Jane Nocona and the late Clara J. Morrison,
unfortunately, are just a few of the many
missing and murdered Indigenous
women and girls."

The Judge is right I think to myself.
But there is so much more to my story.
I stop as we are walking out of the courtroom....
        "We need to do more....
I mutter."
Harrison,

Hazel,
and Rachel stop beside me and the rest of the
courtroom watches...
A reporter steps up to me and asks what I said.
She puts the microphone close to my mouth.
    "We need to do more,"
I say louder.
    "No family should have to beg the police
for help.
And no little girl like Hazel should have to live
five years of her childhood without her mother!"
I start to shake,
but I keep talking...
    "I hope that others will search for the missing
and find them.
Trafficking victims may seem invisible,
but there are signs.
Don't ignore the signs.
Call for help.
I hope for closure for families.
They need and deserve to know what has happened
to their loved ones!
Many loved ones are addicts.
They matter and need help.
You don't give up someone you love!
My foster family did not give up and neither will I!"
I look around.
The crowd is still.
They seem to be looking into my soul.

I am seen.

I nod and continue walking out of the room with
Hazel,

Harrison,

and Rachel close by.

After leaving the courthouse,
the world has changed.
I have changed...

That Night ☾ *Jane Nocona*
April 13, 2029

We go back to Harrison's.
I feel safe there.
That night,
I stand with Hazel outside and
stare up at the sky.
It is dark.
There are small metallic stars
sprinkled all
over the wide-
open sky.
A pink moon is rising...
a symbol of a new beginning.
I have hope.
I have hope because
even though I experienced evil,
I also experienced good...
I know it's out there.
The Henderson's showed me that,
and so did Harrison,
Rachel,
and most of all,
Hazel.

I hope for better laws and legislation
to help protect
the Indigenous people.
I hope for empathy.
I hope for all of the Indigenous women
and girls who never made it home.

I start crying again.
I cry more than I cried when I first
experienced violence when I was twelve.
I cry more than when I was buying a cure
for the pain the first time.
I cry more than when I was forced to leave
the Henderson family who helped me more
than anyone ever has.
I cry more than when I fell into the dark
underworld of sex trafficking.
I cry more than when I found a way out.
I cry because I got justice.
But most of all I cry because I
                     am
                          still
                                alive.

Hope ☾ Jane
April 13, 2029

May the unsolved get solved...
May the missing be found
and brought back home to
their families,
friends,
and communities.
May the murdered be found and
their cases be solved.
May the trafficked be identified,
rescued,
and brought home back to where
they belong.
May justice finally be served.

Seen

This is me.
I am a daughter.
I am a mother.
I am a girlfriend.
I am a friend.
I am somebody.
I AM NOKOMIS NAGUA.
I am whole,
and I am seen....

45

Say Her Name

Liyah Adams
Destinee Atencio
Rhonda Anderson
Antionette Bernhardt
Jasalin Left Hand Bull
Happy Charles
Jennifer Catcheway
Cante Carpenter
Anthonette Cayedito
Justine Cochrane
Ottawa County Jane Doe
Mary Johnson (Davis)
Mossleigh Jane Doe
Stormy Spotted Elk
Samantha Fidder
Amanda Green
Skye Greenway
Ashley Loring Heavyrunner
Jaiden Whirlwind Horse
Cherisse Houle

Selena Not Afraid
Luta Apahroe
Mary Begay
Alina Bartolon
Cheyenne Cross
Jermain Charlo
Jessica Marie Campbell
Heather Cameron
Cleveland County Jane Doe
Nicole Daniels
Burlington County Jane Doe
Harris County Jane Doe
Melissa Estoy
Summer Day
Reatha May Finkbonner
Andrea Gus
Priscilla Gould
TaNeesha S. Holiday
Bonnie Jack
Jayden Harlan

Lindsay Jackson

Azraya Ackabee-Kokopenace

Lamikah Lozier

Shannon Licht-Morsette

Ariel Ofield

Jessica Peters

Aniyah Perez

Maria Alicia Figueroa Ramirez

Angelica Sandoval

Anne Schuster

Diane Stewart

Cheryl Long Soldier

Lena Scott

Alberta Stahi

Gizhe Legarde

Vanessa Lee

Emily Morgan

Justice Michelle

Neoganae Presbury

Holly Painter

Owé White Plume

Pepta Redhair

Christina Leah

Henny Scott

Elaine Smallcanyon

Hattie Olivia-Good Soldier

Antoinette Scholme

and too many more...

Throughout my research for this project, I came across many cases.

Acknowledgements

The creation of *Pink Moon Rising; Pieces of Jane* wouldn't have been possible without the help of a lot of excellent and talented people. First and foremost, I want to thank my mom and dad, Stacey Skold and Mark Hutchings, for being my mom and dad as well as for making me the person I am today. My dad pointed out the pink moon one night at a memorable campfire-I will always remember that. He also took the photograph for the cover and helped with the cover design. My mom helped a lot with the edits and ideas to make this book the book it could be. I really enjoy going to coffeehouses with you! I live for those times! To my lovely sister Hathaway Skold Hutchings, thank you for helping me through this challenging process and for being my sister! To my extended family, thank you for all of your support. To Julia Ramsay, thank you for being my friend and critique/writing partner, I really appreciate you. To Tami Maytum, thank you for being the best speech and drama coach and editor. To Jeff Donahue, thank you for being one of the greatest teachers I've ever had, for being so encouraging, and looking at a few parts of the early drafts. And to all of the other aspiring authors who have supported "bookish.halsten", thank you. Love you lots!

Selected Sources

Aljazeera, "The Search: Missing and Murdered Indigenous Women | Fault Lines," https://www.youtube.com/watch?v=mdPvoNDfMbA

Dressember, "How Are Foster Youth and Former Foster Youth More Susceptible to Human Trafficking," https://www.dressember.org/blog/fosteryouth

Freedom United, "Why Traffickers Go After Native American Women," https://www.freedomunited.org/news/why-traffickers-go-after-native-american-women/

NPR, "Police in Many U.S. Cites Fail to Track Murdered, Missing Indigenous Women," https://www.npr.org/2018/11/15/667335392/police-in-many-u-s-cities-fail-to-track-murdered-missing-indigenous-women

MeganMichaelPhotography

Halsten Sköld Hutchings is a Senior in High School. *Pink Moon Rising* is her debut novel, which she started her Sophomore year. She has always loved books and writing. They are more than a hobby, they are her friends.